WHEN THE ANGELS SAY AMEN

VERA LUCIA LIMA

Publisher:

Inspiring Publishers

P.O. Box 159, Calwell, ACT Australia 2905

Email: publishaspg@gmail.com

http://www.inspiringpublishers.com

National Library of Australia Cataloguing-in-Publication

Entry Author: LIMA, VERA LUCIA

Title: **When the Angel Say Amen**/VERA LUCIA LIMA

Subtitle: **A Spiritual Journey through Cherokee Oppression, Betrayal,
Survival and Love**

ISBN: 9781521516645 (pbk)

Subjects: Native American & Aboriginal
Cherokee Indians – fiction

Cover Illustration/Artwork by David K. Rees

Layout and Graphic Design by Telma Blaiotta

A Word to the Reader

As a psychic, the contents of this book were revealed and channeled through my spiritual dreams. I was able to record and write down the episodes as they were revealed in my native Portuguese language and then piece them together to produce this story.

I had no previous knowledge of the individuals involved or have ever studied the Cherokee people or these times — two hundred years ago.

I would ask the reader to approach this work with an open mind and heart as I can offer no rational explanation to the origin of this perplexing scenario.

In dedication, I would like to thank God for this ability and spiritual connection, my parents and my children, whom I love and whose support was critical to me to fulfill my spiritual mission.

"Love only has one eye—not two."
A Cherokee saying

Vera Lucia Lima

Contents

Oppressive Times

The Native North American Cherokee Indians lived with pain, conflict, and sadness.

In the early 1800's, many indigenous people who lived and hunted across America were persecuted by the recent arrivals from Europe, who saw them as being in the way of their progress in occupying *their* country. The white man regarded them as ignorant savages, but they were very far from that. They were careful conservationists; they respected the land and the wildlife to provide themselves with food and shelter.

White Wolf was the chief of all the Cherokee tribes. He called the three Cherokee nations together to a tribal council meeting to discuss the situation. However, soon after the meeting, the U.S. Army, under Captain Harold, brutally invaded their territory with cannons and rifles.

During the invasion, the hot atmosphere of the day became filled with smoke and the acrid smell of gunpowder, and there was much death and suffering.

Mother Nature witnessed this sad fate of the "Children of the Earth".

During the fighting that day, at the height of the battle, Captain Harold noticed a mature Indian woman called

Aiyana. She was standing defiantly right in the middle of the battle! Her long silver hair fell over her shoulder, down her decorated tunic. Her face was strong, determined, and defiant, with the relentless gaze and fixation of a spiritual healer and a focused warrior.

The matriarch had heard the cries and witnessed the deaths of her people for so long, yet she remained serene. She held a clay bowl containing herbs and a woven fabric lain over it.

Captain Harold was quite astonished as he watched this woman in the middle of all this chaos — but suddenly, an eagle wheeling above her diverted his attention. Returning his gaze to the woman, he noticed that the fabric had slipped and that it had been hiding something that shone and glinted amongst the herbs. He pointed his rifle to Aiyana.

She stood her ground and seemed to have no fear as he approached her. A shiver went up her spine as she faced a great spiritual test, and she ignored him and maintained her hard, cold stare. She turned her back on him and walked to a nearby tent, one that was larger than the others. Before entering, she turned and shouted, "You are an Enemy of Life" in Cherokee at Captain Harold. As she shouted, she gestured with both her arms wide, and something glinted as it fell to the ground from the bowl.

He followed it and saw an amazing sight — she had dropped a sparkling diamond and a piece of gold! He picked them up and held them in his hands. He could not believe his eyes! He suddenly thought, *What luck! In addition to the victory over the Indians, I am now sure that they must have more treasure like this, and I will have a chance to now find the place where they hide it all! For some reason, I could not bring myself to shoot this ignorant Indian woman, there was something about her eyes that threatened me and I felt almost paralyzed. I have never seen such bravery — like a great warrior, unlike some of my own men.*

Aiyana had seemed to paralyze the captain's trigger finger. He now followed her into the large tent, which was the home of Morning Flower, a young Indian woman. She was in labor and waiting for assistance to give birth. Captain Harold stood there, his rifle pointed at Aiyana, surprised to see such a scene. Morning Flower was screaming with pain, unaware of him standing by her side with his rifle now pointed at her. Aiyana approached the captain, took his rifle, and placed it on the floor. He froze, astonished that he had actually allowed this Indian woman to disarm him. He remained perplexed by this and stood away from it. He felt the diamond and the gold in his pocket. He could not speak their language, but thought, *How can I make this Indian show me where all the gold is?* He knew that this old woman was unusual, and with her fearless and brazen attitude, she was challenging his authority and power. He knew that all she wanted to do was to help with the birth, even if it cost her own life.

It was the first time he had ever surrendered to a woman! he realized. Stroking his beard, he concluded, *Yes! Now everything makes sense. The old woman was taking gifts to the Cherokee chief White Wolf's daughter! This has to be the truth. The other Indian nations had said that there was gold in the Cherokee territory.*

He controlled his excitement, watching the young woman's painful birth and looking closely at her face. For a moment, he was touched by what he saw. He remembered his present wife who could not give him children, his empty marriage, and his family that despised all of his misfortunes.

Captain Harold did not like white women. He liked and fell for Native Americans. Since he was an army captain, he could never reveal that he was involved with a mestiza (half- caste) named Salish. Everyone had thought he was still widowed from his first marriage. Salish was the daughter of a white father and a Native American mother who had been captured by the Sioux Indian tribe.

Captain Harold could not have a family life because his relationship with Salish was not socially acceptable and he lived away from his officers. His family was against his bad-tempered behavior, and he was embarrassed by Salish's indigenous ancestry.

Captain Harold's mother-in-law raised Elvira, his only daughter, because she did not approve of her living with him because of his mestiza wife.

Meanwhile, the killing and endless tragedy continued outside, with pain, suffering, and cries. And, at the same time, Morning Flower was drained of all her strength due to her screaming, and Aiyana worked hard to facilitate the birth. The young mother-to-be fainted because of her weakness and the emotion generated by all the noise of the fighting. Amongst all this chaos, the baby arrived into the world, receiving grace and the breath of life. And Captain Harold witnessed this special moment. Fixated with his mission to kill all the Cherokees but having just witnessed the birth of another, he decided that he would stop the attack.

He was reminded of an old Cherokee saying: "Even a snake didn't attack when witnessing a birth".

It was a difficult birth, one that was to have fatal consequences due to the battle for Morning Flower.

Aiyana cut the umbilical cord and cleaned the baby with herbs and water, swaddling her in the white cloths she had brought.

At that very moment, a stray bullet came from outside, whistling through the tent, and hit the mother in the chest, seriously injuring her. Blood started to gush profusely from her body, and she died quickly.

Captain Harold immediately went outside the tent and shouted the soldiers to cease fire. A nearby soldier, whose bullet had probably hit the poor mother, didn't understand why the captain was there, and asked him, "Captain what were you doing in that tent? We were worried and looking for you to advise us about a withdrawal."

But, on hearing the cries of the baby, he entered the tent, and realizing that he had probably killed the young mother, pointed his rifle at Aiyana. She grabbed the baby and held it to her pounding chest. The captain, having witnessed the death and now the actions of the soldier, screamed, "Cursed soldier! Put down your gun. Who gave you orders to kill that young woman?"

With a forced and challenging smile, the soldier replied, "Captain, your orders were to kill all the Cherokees."

"Yes, soldier, what you saw here is an exception. Don't ever speak of what you have seen here."

Captain Harold was surprised and worried about being caught by one of his men, but on the other hand, he was happy about their victory and his "little discovery". Now, he would have access to all the gold in the Cherokee territory through the old woman and the newborn daughter of the Cherokee chief. He kept the diamond and gold in his pocket. It'd be a secret he would not reveal to anyone.

Thinking quickly, he took a piece of paper from his pocket and made a note.

"Sergeant James, take this Indian lady and the baby to this hiding place at this army-guarded reservation. Keep them as hostages and be careful. I want them both alive and well. Understood?"

"Yes, captain. I will follow your orders to the letter, even if I don't understand them."

"Soldier, you should keep your comments and judgments to yourself. Your job is to do what I say without question. Now, get out of my sight, you inquisitive idiot!"

Captain Harold's blood boiled. He felt annoyed at being challenged by the soldier. The baby cried and mourned the absence of her mother. Her soul was in pain and she cried for love.

Aiyana, although tired and battered by the war, held her firmly with all the love of a grandmother and the matriarch of her tribe. She realized that Captain Harold had taken both the diamond and the gold. Her mind raced. She could predict that she and the baby would be taken hostages to make the chief reveal where their gold and gems were hidden.

Aiyana glanced thankfully at Captain Harold and spoke. He nodded. Although he was unable to understand her language, he understood what she meant.

Captain Harold was happy and lit a cigar, congratulating his men for killing so many Cherokees. Some were also taken as hostages. Ironically, it was then that one of his sergeants told him that the Cherokee chief and many of his tribe had managed to evade the attack by escaping to the mountains. They had apparently used a ceremony with a smoky fire and herbs, and after chanting, they had apparently just disappeared! When the smoke cleared, chief White Wolf had vanished.

Captain Harold got annoyed. "Adams, you're irritating me with your nonsense. Your incompetence amazes me. Are you hallucinating? Are you telling me that White Wolf is some kind of a magician?"

Sergeant Adams replied, "Captain, I don't know if what he did was witchcraft, but I saw it with my own eyes. The earth just seemed to swallow him up."

"Sergeant, so the White Wolf is a mystic and nobody can get close to him or he disappears? I don't allow crazy people under my command."

The captain managed to remain composed before his men. "The events in the chief's tent — surrendering to Aiyana, sparing her and a newborn child's life — he kept to himself."

The soldiers left as quickly as possible. He would make up a good excuse to explain White Wolf's escape to the colonel. Victory was easy for them because they used guns against bows and arrows — and even against skilled Cherokee archers, the outcome was inevitable.

Mother Nature had witnessed these dark moments. The Great Spirit was full of sorrow at the pain and suffering caused by the conflict.

Captain Harold Sees His Victims

Aiyana kept the child warm on her chest, conveying love and trust. Sergeant James screamed at her, "Indian, climb into this wagon with that baby and don't let it cry. If you don't obey, I will throw you both off the next cliff. I have no mercy for ignorant Indians."

The sergeant pointed his gun toward Aiyana and indicated to the wagon. She did not fully understand, but she climbed into the wagon and kept the baby from crying by having it suck on her finger, hoping to keep her quiet and not irritate or upset the solider further. She just didn't know what she would do when this strategy no longer worked and the baby became hungry. She thought it was a good time to send heartfelt prayers and spoke to the Great Spirit, "Great Spirit, may your will be done. If I must die, please save the life of White Wolf's daughter. I know I was spared, and that I faced the captain to be saved from death. Let her live. I think many Cherokees from my tribe are gone. I regret that my brother White Wolf had to witness his son getting shot and killed before I was called to help with his daughter's birth. If indeed I have to be the mother of the White Wolf's daughter, please give me a sign of your will to deal with this painful destiny."

"The air was tense; the sergeant irritable and hostile." He thought that he had all the power in his hands, and since it would be easier to disobey his orders and dirty his hands with innocent blood, he hoped that the baby would cry. He studied the Indian woman as they travelled — her silence and serenity disturbed him.

Hours passed and nothing happened. He was amazed at this woman's strength, her willpower, and being unmoved by his threats, her apparent lack of fear. What was this woman made of?

The horses trotted along the rough road at a good pace. Unexpectedly, the sergeant's eyes started to close. The gun, resting on his lap and pointing at Aiyana and the baby, slipped down.

The sun, starting to set, bidding farewell to the day, emitted a golden, yellow, and orange glow. Aiyana noticed the sergeant and silently asked the Great Spirit to help keep him dozing. Finally, feeling exhausted, he dozed off.

It was then that the Spirit of Mother Earth, Pachamama, revealed herself to Aiyana as a Native American woman, wearing an emerald green robe embroidered with golden gems. The Queen of the Forest had a sparkling tiara of precious stones and colorful feathers in her long, black hair. Her angelic face conveyed her love, which she communicated.

"Daughter of the Earth, take care of "White Moon" as she will be called by the Cherokees. White Moon has the Divine Mother's blessing." Mother Earth's voice sounded like a sweet song that could be enjoyed like the purest of honey.

As she spoke, there was the rumble of loud thunder. Aiyana's vision now became as a dream and was taken over by a large and pure ice-covered mountain.

From high in the mountain, the Great Spirit's voice could be heard loudly.

"Daughter of the Earth, prepare White Moon for she will bring peace between the Cherokees and the white man. Don't fear the white man. You have Pachamama and Me by your side. No harm will come to you. Be strong and courageous! Children of the Light will resist all evil and be victorious in the end."

Pachamama appeared on the right side of the mountain and bowed to the Great Spirit. She raised her arms and then the Queen of the Forest hugged the mountain. On her long fingers a large diamond ring glinted, given to her by the earth.

At this point, Aiyana was awakened by White Moon, who was still sucking her finger in search of food, the white cloth around her soaked in urine. Sergeant James also awoke as the wagon gave a large jolt.

The sergeant was still amazed that the baby was still sucking on the Indian woman's finger and hadn't cried during the long journey! How was this possible? How did this woman achieve this? What was her secret? He stared down at Aiyana's feet and thought, This Indian takes care of herself. *She is wearing beautifully decorated animal skin moccasins — where does this knowledge come from if they are ignorant?* He contemplated Aiyana's pride of appearance and the hand-work that must have gone into the decoration of her clothes. White women never put this degree of work and pride into their appearance. He admired her long silver and white hair. Wrinkles marked her face with wisdom. Her clothes were made of unbleached fabric, all handmade, with orange and brown geometric designs, and her shawl covered her nurturing arms. He wanted to know who she was but realized that she did not speak English. If these Indians were so ignorant, as he believed, where then did all the knowledge of complex geometric designs on her tunic and shawl come from? The sergeant shook his head from side to side, thinking, *I will have to stop these thoughts, I must be going crazy!*

As they approached their destination, Sergeant James became aggressive again. They were approaching the army run Cheyenne Indian reservation.

Aiyana thanked the Great Spirit and Mother Earth. White Moon was hungry. Yet, despite being wet, she was warm and fed by Aiyana's faith. Aiyana got down and took White Moon to be breastfed by a Cheyenne Indian mother and observed the Cheyenne way of life. She knew that living with the white man now would be a serious challenge for her.

How was she going to survive without her tribal family? Her thoughts were far away when she felt someone touching her right arm. The young boy spoke to her in Cherokee. "Who are you? Welcome to our Indian reservation. My name is Utah. Can I help you? You must be hungry. I will bring you something to eat."

Aiyana was surprised but cheered by this welcome and felt she was at home. Someone here spoke her language; the Great Spirit was in charge, she knew.

Utah was just twelve years old, with black hair, hazel eyes, and an open and honest smile. He was taken to the Indian reservation when he was seven. All the young Indians had to learn English. They were also forced to become Christians and renounce all the knowledge of their tribe. But Utah knew what to do and was not beaten like the others. He was agreeable by nature, integrating well with everyone, but in his heart, he was a Native American Indian and a Son of the Earth. He wore a protective mask to survive.

Utah quickly brought a bowl with corn and water to Aiyana, and the two of them sat there talking for hours into the night. Next day, they continued to talk together until they saw the cavalry arrive. To Aiyana's great surprise, it was Captain Harold and some of his soldiers. He dismounted, pleased to see that Aiyana had arrived safely.

"Where is the Cherokee baby?" he asked Utah. Utah told him, and both of them walked together to one of the tents. The Indian baby was also safe, the captain was happy to see that. *This is a living legacy that I have as captive here, he thought, but I feel that I should bring Aiyana along with her. I'm lucky I will also have Utah to accompany me. I will take all three captives soon, when the heiress to the Cherokees' gold no longer needs to be nursed. My plan is perfect. Utah speaks English and he will help me understand the Cherokee language. I am the only one who has the keys to this treasure. I may provoke a situation — when the three of them will be permanently in my hands.*

Six months later, the captain put his plan into action.

One day in winter, when the sun was at its highest, Captain Harold arrived at the Cheyenne reservation on an old wagon, wearing a long black robe with a hood that covered much of his face. Without attracting any attention, he pointed his rifle at Utah, Aiyana, and the baby, and covering them and making them lie down in the back of the wagon, took them to a cabin far away.

Utah did not realize that the disguised man was the captain. They arrived at the remote cabin, where wild wolves prowled the area.

Even though they had plenty of food and water, the strong and cold winds made them feel insecure. They suffered with the intense cold, which cut White Moon's fragile lips. At night, you could only hear the sound of the wolves howling. Captain Harold was cautious and had asked a soldier to leave animal skins at the cabin, but these had been all hidden away and locked up. Aiyana, White Moon, and Utah had been left in the cabin for a week on their own when the captain appeared without his disguise, wearing his military uniform. Brazenly, he once again began to lie to gain Aiyana's trust.

With a fake smile, he said, "I was told that the three of you were abducted. One of my soldiers learned where the kidnappers were hiding out and I paid them off. I don't have any obligation to return Indians to the reservation. In fact, many are being sold as slaves to European farmers. What do you think about working in my house if I pay for the three of you? Utah, you already speak English, and Aiyana could take care of the baby and help my wife with the daily chores." Aiyana knew that he was not honest — he had already stolen White Moon's diamond and gold. Yet, he had spared her life, now for the second time. She sensed his treacherous intentions and said so to Utah in Cherokee: "This man is a treacherous spear in our lives. Fate has brought us to him and we should not back away. If we run away, we will be killed or handed over as slaves. So, let it be." Utah lowered his head and agreed with Aiyana, and they told the captain that they would go with him. They left the cabin for the captain's house.

While Aiyana, White Moon, and Utah travelled to Captain Harold's home, the crescent moon, from high in the mountains, witnessed the pain of Cherokee's Shaman (spiritually gifted) chief.

Escape to the High Mountains

White Wolf had sensed through his spiritual power that he should lead his tribe to the Rocky Mountains. He and his brother Amitola had already taken food reserves. Even if the military destroyed their villages, the Cherokee nation would survive this chaos.

White Wolf was thirty-nine years old. "He had big hazel eyes; eyes that turned eagle-like before enemies, seeing through all their evil intentions." He had a proud face with strong rugged features, black hair to his shoulders, and an imposing chest that commanded respect and fear. There was no white man who could challenge him with a knife or a bow and arrow and win. He simply didn't know about guns, but he used his spiritual knowledge to not be caught and killed by the army.

Thanks to his spiritual gift — being a "Shaman" — he was able to see the future. He did not fear evil. After witnessing his son, Tame Bull, and other warriors get killed by guns and cannons from afar, White Wolf prepared a supernatural occurrence and disappeared as two soldiers watched in awe. His brother, Amitola, led his warriors into the high mountains. After a dream, the chief summoned the whole tribe to a meeting. They were all apprehensive about what White Wolf would say, having spiritually learned the death of Tame Bull, his son, Morning Flower, his wife, and the loss of White Moon, his daughter, and Aiyana, his sister and the matriarch of the Cherokees.

The sound of a large bear on the other side of the mountain broke the silence of that moment, and Amitola, carrying a big, broken bow in his hand, stepped into the middle of the circle. "Chief and Cherokee brothers, thanks to the Great Spirit who guided us to this mountain. I thank you for bringing supplies and animal skins to warm the tribe. I feel that your hearts are broken, like this bow and split in half."

"Yes, my heart is in pieces! A large whip has lashed my soul, Amitola. My beloved Morning Flower died from a stray gunshot wound moments after she gave birth to our daughter, aided by our oldest sister, Aiyana. Morning Flower was taken to the Great Spirit and after that, I witnessed the death of my son, Tame Bull. At that same moment, I had to choose between him and our tribe. If I stayed there to defend him, there would not have been time to save our tribe." With those words, nature silenced the strong winds that were coming towards White Wolf, bringing confirmation. The Cherokees gathered around their chief. Amitola, with trembling knees, sank down to the ground, asking the Great Spirit to comfort his own heart as well as that of his brothers and his whole tribe.

"I, Shaman and chief of the Cherokees, have gathered everyone together for a Spiritual Ceremony. Prepare fires, because we will have a gathering for the Great Spirit to bring our warriors to the Light and so that Pachamama, our Mother Earth, may comfort them. After the ceremonies, I will call the tribe to discuss new war strategies."

Humming Bird, a young and pretty Indian girl came up to White Wolf, took his hand and kissed it. "I'm cold," she said,

"I have lost both my parents and this place scares me. I hear there are wolves and big bears on the other side of the mountain. Can I sit on your lap? I am looking for Aiyana, where is she? "Her protective arms were like my mother's."

From the corner of the chief's eye, a tear ran down his cheek. He picked up the little girl and put her in his lap and rocked her on his heaving chest. He was overcome by the great emotion of the moment, the loss of Morning Flower, and his newborn daughter.

"Don't be scared of the big bear, Humming Bird. I will roast him on a big fire if he threatens you. I will break all of his teeth with my strong fists. I will crush his head and make a meal for us. We will take his hide to warm your home on the coldest days." Humming Bird smiled, feeling happy and secure. "Now you go onto Amitola's lap. He knows how to deal with human pain and he can also cure heavy hearts. My brother, Amitola — take care of little Humming Bird. Her spiritual pain is tied to all the pain and loss in the tribe."

"Yes, the Great Spirit gave me the power and wisdom to heal the broken heart. I know that we are very different, but when we work together we complement each other."

White Wolf agreed with his brother's ability to always speak the truth.

"It is not in my nature to cure heartache. Spiritual coldness drives me and makes me clever. I only look for spiritual warmth when I have overcome the cold. Only then can I enjoy the warmth of the sun, life, and the sacred fire. Take this little girl and bring her to a warrior woman with a kind heart, so that she can enjoy the love and warmth of a good Cherokee mother worthy of her heart. Now, prepare the torches, a big fire, and the sacred dances. The rituals will last all night. It is a sacred moment with the Great Spirit."

A New Life for White Moon, Aiyana, and Utah

As they approached the captain's house, the hostages were completely silent. White Moon was the only one who smiled innocently at Captain Harold. The penetrating gaze that she inherited from White Wolf seemed like two black pearls that tried to communicate with the captain's eyes. White Moon was the sole heir of the Cherokee nation. The captain would have to be true to his plans. He could not give in and love the Cherokee baby. His heart would have to be hardened.

An unexpected conflict occurred when Aiyana got off the wagon with White Moon and Utah. Salish, the captain's wife, was in the garden waiting for the group. Surprised and full of emotion, she cried, "Ah, a beautiful Cherokee baby." She rushed over to Aiyana and grabbed the baby from her. The little White Moon got scared and began to cry.

The captain raised his arms and said, "It's good that I brought Aiyana to take care of the girl. I hope that you learn to take care of our daughter. She will be called Samira in honor of my Arabic grandmother. She will have everything and be educated in the American culture. When Elvira comes to visit me; I'll tell her that I have adopted a Cherokee girl. She will just have to accept it."

Salish was a tall and slender Native American with emerald green eyes, the result of the mixture between her white father and her Sioux mother. She had a big smile, rosy complexion, and strong indigenous features. Her hair was black, and she had a well-defined figure. The captain kept her imprisoned at home, away from the eyes of the officers in his regiment.

Salish knew the indigenous code of ethics. You never 'just take' what is not yours. She lowered her head, got herself together, and apologized to Aiyana. She led her new tribal family towards their rooms. They would be assisted by Emma, the captain's black maid, who had been his first wife's faithful servant.

Aiyana realized the pain the captain's wife was going through. She took White Moon because only she knew how to deal with the girl. Once everyone settled into their rooms, Aiyana called Utah.

"Young Utah, I'm in your hands. Tell me everything in our Cherokee language when the captain speaks. I have never heard of mixed blood. The white man does not speak our language. I don't understand the Sioux language. You are the only one who does. Because of the lack of love, the captain's wife grabbed White Moon from my arms as if she were her own daughter." In frustration, Aiyana let out a cry and called out to the Great Spirit. "What cruel fate has brought us to this house. The woman doesn't seem like a bad person, but she took something that wasn't hers."

"Yes, it is true," Utah replied. "Grandmother Aiyana, I want you to know that the captain will adopt White Moon as his daughter."

At that moment, Emma appeared, bringing warm milk, and suggested Aiyana feed White Moon. Aiyana was able to read body language and understood Emma's position within the household. This was the first time she had ever seen or met a black woman. We have different skin, but the same spiritual essence, she thought. We are sisters of the heart. As a gesture of gratitude, she nodded to Emma as she came closer to White Moon, who was waiting for food in her little crib that Emma had prepared.

The captain's living room was ornate but cold. It was full of American-style mahogany furniture. The china cabinet was filled with exquisite crystal that sparkled with the flicker of candles on the table. Dinner was then served by Emma, and the captain gave orders.

"Salish, since you do nothing in this house, you need to learn the Cherokee language from Utah who speaks English. Learn through Aiyana what she is saying and teach them our customs. For example, as Indians, they should always eat with Emma in the kitchen. I don't want closer contact with them, only with our daughter Samira."

Salish ironically looked at an oil painting on the wall of the King of England and said, "What would your family say if they saw this house? A Cherokee baby kidnapped by an American army captain, who lives with his unrecognized Dakota Sioux Indian wife who was not accepted by either Indians or white people?"

The captain was furious and thumped his fist on the table, knocking a porcelain dish to the floor, smashing it and emptying the food. He got up and slapped Salish across the side of her face. "Accept your fate and don't complain. I paid your price to your father. If you were sold to Europeans, it would have been worse. Your American Indian beauty interests me. Learn to care for Samira; she will be strong and beautiful. I want her to speak our language and that of the Cherokee Indians. In time, you will also teach her to speak the language of the Sioux Indians. What luck that Utah also knows how to speak these two native languages. I want to better understand these people and where all of their knowledge comes from. Maybe Samira will help me to understand the Native Americans. White Wolf will never take Samira from me. I will use her to find out where White Wolf hides the gold in the Cherokee territory."

Salish raised her head and tried to recover from the blow to her face. For a moment, she felt disgusted by the monster who was always claiming to be her husband. Her blood ran hot and she wiped the tears that were falling down her beautiful face that was constantly abused by the captain. He had a horrible temper, and after going out with his soldiers often came home drunk. Salish thought, *They say that Indians are ignorant, but I remember my mother say that the Sioux Indians don't mistreat their wives, let alone beat them.* Salish recovered quickly with her indigenous strength, staring at the captain, and screamed:

"The Great Spirit will punish you for all of your abuse. White Wolf is feared by all indigenous nations. They even say he is a Shaman."

"I am not afraid of White Wolf, Salish," he replied. "I have modern guns, and the United States military weaponry will always win, there is no doubt about that. In time, you will see that they will give up their treasure. Any parent, even if he doesn't know the child, would give it up to have his daughter back. I was the only one to witness Samira's birth. I will not return the heiress, I just want the gold — and I will get it, you will see, my dear."

Salish humiliated, went to Samira's room, and when she held the child to her chest, accepting her as her adopted daughter, she gained some spiritual comfort.

Aiyana heard the screams that came from the dining room. She didn't need to speak English to understand that she was in the home of her worst enemy. She slept with a sad and tired heart.

White Wolf Plants Love

After performing the ceremonies, White Wolf went to his camp and thought of his sister Aiyana. He slowly relaxed eventually and fell asleep. He was able to communicate with her in his mind. They had both promised that if evil ever separated them, they would, with the help of the Great Spirit, make a spiritual connection through their dreams.

White Wolf was thus able to meet Aiyana and was shocked to meet his daughter who had been kidnapped along with her. Aiyana told him everything that had happened since the day the tribe was attacked by the captain. Tears poured from the great warrior's eyes. He knew how to overcome his pain with love. He watched as his daughter slept and noticed how much she looked like Morning Flower. The chief thanked the Great Spirit for giving him his spiritual gift and power that allowed him to see and admire his daughter. The full moon emitted a strong silver light that bathed his daughter's cozy room. She was the heir of his heart. Since the Great Spirit had allowed his daughter to be kidnapped by the white man, he would have to be stronger and more experienced to fight for her life and try to understand the lessons that he could learn from the loss of almost his entire family.

White Wolf sensed that Captain Harold intended to kill all the Cherokees and negotiate the life of his daughter for the location of all their gold.

Aiyana knew that she was sleeping. Yet, through their dreams, the meeting with her brother was very real and unique. She asked White Wolf to tell her other brother Amitola about the kidnapping. She needed to heal the pain of being separated from the tribe, and she could not make spiritual contact with him through her dreams. White Wolf kissed Aiyana's face and affectionately hugged and kissed his daughter. The night witnessed the spiritual mystery of the dream world, where the impossible does not exist. It worked for souls most in need of Divine Help.

After spiritually meeting his daughter, White Wolf returned to his physical body. When he woke up, he tried to calm down and overcome all that he had heard from Aiyana.

He thought, *I will need clarity and to keep my feet on the ground. I will have to be more cunning than the foxy white man to get my daughter back.*

With that thought, White Wolf walked to the fire. He contemplated the 'grandfather fire' and asked for enlightenment and wisdom from the Great Spirit to guide his tribe. The weapons of the white man were unknown to him, and therefore, he had a great disadvantage. He noticed that everyone was in their tents, and he took a blanket and covered himself while a cold breeze came up from the mountain to refresh and give him new life. He was interrupted by Amitola.

"This is the first time I have seen hope in your eyes since your son and Morning Flower were taken away. I see happiness in your eyes and imagine that the Great Spirit let you visit Aiyana through your dreams. How was it?"

"I wish that you also had my gift of time travel and to see the truth," White Wolf replied, his voice weighed by emotions. White Moon, my daughter, is alive and she is beautiful like her mother Morning Flower. Aiyana needs your help because she and my daughter are being held hostage by the white man. He has guns in his home. Call all the Indian chiefs for a meeting on the next full moon at our usual place — where the white man has never set foot."

"I understand and feel that the white man's leader and benefactor is confused. He wants to give land to all the indigenous nations and wants all of them to surrender. His heart is in the right place, but unfortunately, he will be betrayed by those who pretend to obey his orders. There will be no peace while there is still the desire to steal the yellow metal and natural resources. It would be easier to send those who have not been killed to arid and baron lands where we will have no rights. They have no respect for us."

"The war has already begun with the suffering and death of our fellow tribesmen and the disappearance of White Moon and Aiyana."

"Don't forget that in order to be a negotiator, I learned to speak the native language of the other chiefs. Although it has been a long time since I have seen them, I still have good friendly relationships with the Chickasaws, Shawnees, and some other chiefs that I will not mention." Amitola, the negotiator and warrior, felt a chill go through his whole body when he mentioned that difficult meeting. He felt fearful. Was his brother's proposal madness or courage? For a moment, he was in doubt.

Noticing his brother's reaction to this, White Wolf raised his voice, "I'm not afraid of being killed by any of them. War is the only time that our enemies unite to save themselves. I have my weapons ready."

The fresh breeze from the mountains blew strongly. Amitola felt uplifted and more aware. Relieved by his brother's answer, he asked, "How do you communicate with the other chiefs from the border? They are very dangerous, and I wouldn't dare meet with them. I prefer to communicate with Mother Nature and learn about her ways to heal our tribe's spiritual and physical ills."

"We share the same blood, but we are very different at the core. I left all fear in the bowels of Mother Earth when I came into this world. I am a Shaman, and the warrior chiefs know that I can travel through dreams. I can figure out what the white man is doing. I do not have any guns. My weapons are my skills as a warrior. I can travel through a conscious spiritual dimension and even if they kill me, I will still continue guiding White Moon and the Cherokees. Life will go on! The challenge is not to turn over the yellow metal, but to defend our right to live the life that they want to take from us, this life that the Great Spirit and Mother Earth have given to us."

After hearing such an eloquent affirmation of the truth, a tear fell from Amitola's eye. He began to think of his mission to convene the chiefs for the meeting. The next day, before the roosters awoke, he used his spiritual gifts to talk to the animals and called the great master eagle. He asked her to send White Wolf's invitation to the other indigenous leaders.

White Wolf was walking around the mountain, thinking, when little Humming Bird, accompanied by her foster mother, appeared with a young sun colored coyote pup in her hands. She gave the coyote to him as if it were a present, happy to have found someone to take care of it. For a minute, the warrior thought, *I wonder if I will be alive to see White Moon as happy as Humming Bird*. He petted the little coyote and then joined the other Indians to hunt deer and wild turkeys.

Elvira's Return

Time passed and White Moon turned three. Aiyana joined Salish to keep the 'enemy' close to her. Thanks to Aiyana's guidance, Salish was now not beaten by the captain. He sent young Utah to the English school at a nearby reservation, imposing the American culture through other Indians. He knew everything that happened in the indigenous communities. He duly translated what the other Indians said and gained even more of the captain's trust. He had a gift for understanding and talking with other indigenous nations, and he tried to hear everything that was important. Many Indians, because of him, survived the attacks from the soldiers on their villages.

Meanwhile, Aiyana came to accept that she would have to live isolated from her people. White Moon was a great comfort in the darkest days. The difficulty for her was to accept White Moon with the name Samira. She said her name with difficulty, to not upset the captain by saying the little girl's name in her native language.

The captain increasingly tried to gain Aiyana's trust. At the right time, he would get the information from her about where White Wolf had hidden the gold.

One day, he went to White Moon's room to hold her on his lap and cuddle her. He often felt some guilt for taking White Wolf's place. But his ambition was stronger than his heart, and it was this ambition that drove him. *I can't take her into my heart, he thought, because, when I lay my hands on the gold in the end, she will be my financial liberation. Samira will never know the truth.*

One morning, the warm sun heralded the arrival of spring through Mother Nature, with the trees and flowers sprouting new growth, and the birds busily going about their business, but they were not happy — they reflected the sadness of the People of the Earth — and few could interpret it.

Outside the house, horse's hooves stirred up the dust on the road, bringing a surprise. Elvira, the captain's daughter, and her husband arrived at the captain's home. They were no friends of Mother Nature or Native Americans. Elvira was a cold and calculating woman. Tall with a light complexion; she had an emotionless face and cold blue eyes that only conveyed evil. She was often sad because she was not a man and therefore not accepted in the US Army. Women were expected to wear a skirt, but when she wanted to frustrate her father, she wore men's clothing and a military uniform.

The captain opened the door, and very surprised at what he saw, raised an eyebrow. Elvira had married one of the most feared colonels that he knew in the US Army, one who was much older than he was.

"Don't just stand there," Elvira said, noticing his surprise. "Aren't you going to invite us in? I want to introduce you to my new husband, Colonel Phillip." The colonel coolly reached out his hand to greet the captain.

"Why didn't you tell me of your intended visit? It's quite unexpected! Why, after so many years, have you come back to your father's home?"

Salish was carrying White Moon in her arms, who played with her braids. Not knowing what was happening, shocked and suspicious by this unexpected visit, Salish held her breath.

"My father, what I see answers my questions. I had heard of your marriage to a mestiza, and that's why I decided to stay away for all of these years. I am Emma's daughter's godmother, and she secretly asked me to swear that I would never come here to your home. Even worse is that you actually have an Indian hidden in your house and you treat her like your daughter. I didn't think I would ever see anything so ridiculous. How have you been able to hide this calamity from the Army?"

Immediately after those highly offensive words, Salish took White Moon to the servant's quarters, where Aiyana, deeply saddened after hearing the conversation, sat with her head down. The captain shouted for Salish, and she meekly returned to her husband's side.

Emma watched the whole scene. The servant was saddened and very embarrassed by the confession and tried to overcome what had been shattered after her daughter had told the family's secret. The maid went to the kitchen and quickly made some aromatic tea and served the visitors some fresh home baked bread and apple pie on an English silver tray in the main room. Salish put her head down, feeling worthless and insecure. Her blood boiled inside her.

Colonel Phillip mocked her as he twisted his moustache. He looked at Salish's young and beautiful figure as she poured the tea, and stood up, saying, "Dear captain, I can see why you were so attracted to this Indian that you were willing to risk being removed from your post. I'm sorry, but I don't stay where Indians mix with the white man. It is unethical for me to stay here in your home. I will leave your daughter here, if she wants to stay. Oh, and you are lucky because we are now all family here, and don't worry, I will not tell the Army about this. You can thank Elvira for this, but I want you to know my silence comes at a price. American Indians can be very beautiful." Laughing, he began to leave.

The captain realized that the colonel had evil intentions, and he felt the urge to pick up the gun in his office and kill the smirking colonel. With great difficulty, the captain managed to pull himself together.

"My daughter, please make yourself at home if you want to stay. We have so much to talk about. Otherwise, if you decide to leave with your husband, I'll understand. After all, you have never explained your life to me. You have always done what you have wanted to do — on your own."

"Father, I want you to know that my husband has every right to leave this house to honor his title, of which he is so proud. As for me, I'll stay. I think you owe me an explanation about this Cherokee baby."

Colonel Phillip affectionately kissed his wife, turned, and without saying a word to the others, pompously stomped off. He was so angry at having to leave without his wife that he collided with Utah, who was coming back from the reservation, and they both fell to the floor. The colonel, already angry, shouted as he got up: "This place is a nightmare! There are Indians everywhere in this house." He hit Utah as he was getting up, and then kicked him hard with his big boots. He continued to kick him all over his body without mercy. Bent double from the pain, a trickle of blood emerged from Utah's nose. He had no idea what was happening or why he was receiving this beating from the colonel. Aiyana, hearing his cries, ran to help him. Emma — who loved young Utah like the son she never had, who, in her spare time, would take the Bible and teach him words of wisdom — joined Aiyana to help Utah, and together with Salish, they managed to get him into the servant's room at the back of the house.

The colonel brushed himself off, mounted his horse, and rode off at great speed. After the dust settled, the captain invited Elvira into his study and closed the door.

"Who do you think you are? You show up at my house unannounced, married to one of the most feared men in America."

"I am in complete control of my own life," Elvira replied angrily.

He thought about telling her to leave. "Elvira! You have always exasperated me. Your mother was a saint to put up with you until her dying day. Contrary to what you may think, I took this baby to raise because she is a very special Indian, and I have given her the name Samira. She is not just any Indian. Oh no, she is the daughter and heir to all the gold in the Cherokee territory! At the right time, I'll negotiate for her life with White Wolf, the Cherokee Indian chief."

Elvira after her father's startling revelation, understood the situation — how she could benefit from it, and what it could mean for her. She was amazed and laughed at her father's cleverness. "Oh! I am so glad that I inherited your foxiness. Congratulations! I am your ally and heir to the gold. Knowing this, I will be able to live with the differences and racial conflicts in the family."

White Wolf Brings Leaders Together

Mother Nature contemplated the morning star, which sent crystal white rays of light onto the mountaintops. With it, all the other indigenous leaders came together for this important meeting.

White Wolf, covered in animal hide, feathered leggings, and with a shaved head, introduced himself with a wolf-like howl. He thanked everyone for coming. Amitola came to the main tent with long, smoking peace pipes made of clay and offered them to all the leaders. They acknowledged and greeted each other. Owing to White Wolf's spiritual gift of communicating through dreams and his ease of speaking in other native languages, he was able to communicate with all of them and invite them to a War Council.

After observing each leader for a long time with his eagle eye, White Wolf chose Spotted Jaguar and Golden Eagle to lead the Tribal Council. Golden Eagle knew how to negotiate and was naturally charismatic. He could influence others when he believed in the mission for which he was chosen. Spotted Jaguar was strong, fearless, and could easily communicate with the white man. White Wolf lit the big bonfire and the first peace pipe, and silently looked into the sacred fire.

He began to speak, "Warriors of Mother Earth, I thank the Great Spirit for everyone being here on the mountain. Keep in your hearts everything that I say through the Great Spirit." The Shaman Chief changed his tone of voice when the Great Spirit, through the fire and after the meditation, revealed to all what was happening and what was to come for the indigenous nations. Unfortunately, it wasn't a painless or easy encounter. "As a shaman and chief of the Cherokees, I must warn you to prepare your hearts to see our people massacred in a mass slaughter. The blood of our people will be shed without pity or compassion from the white man with his fire weapons. I have watched my son getting killed. Morning Flower was hit in the heart after the birth of our daughter, and White Moon is now being held hostage by a brutal army officer. Desire for the yellow metal will be the great cause of a war. The white man will steal our fertile land and send us to lifeless lands without vegetation. There will be no respect for our tribal families. Our women will be raped by white men. Our babies will not be respected and will be killed even while they are still in their mothers' wombs. Our homes will be burnt and we will not be allowed to live where the Great Spirit gave us life."

Disgusted, one of the tribal chiefs shouted, "Why have you summoned us? You could not tell us anything worse than this!"

White Wolf continued, "We can still change the sad fate of our nations. Yet, there will be traitors and thieves who will not listen to orders and not comply with the peace treaties. Unfortunately, the traitors will divide our union, so that they can rule the tribes and take the place of leaders. They will sell information for food, and we will be ripped from our territory by force. The leader of the white man has enough weapons to get all of us off our lands.

He will also be betrayed by his war allies, and nobody will really know for sure who started the war. There will be complete chaos, and innocent blood will be shed on both sides. But we will be the hardest hit, punished, and forcefully taken, without any fair hearings by the white man.

"Don't trust his plans to not attack. It is not enough to just shoot bows and arrows or set traps in the forest and wait for the white man to strike first. I ask you chiefs to remain united and forget your personal disagreements because this is a very serious time, and we must do everything to fulfill the agreement with the white man's leader. We can't fail from lack of character. Remember, they think we are ignorant savages. The truth is and with the Daughter of Time, the white man will destroy Mother Nature."

All the leaders were shocked by his prophecy. After a while, White Wolf broke the silence.

"I must warn you, this is the first and last of our meetings. Everything will be based on friendship, love, and an example we will leave for other nations."

Frightened by White Wolf's pessimism, one of the leaders became angry and stood up, shouting, "I will not accept this bitter fate that we are hearing." White Wolf asked him to calm down and then spoke:

"Unfortunately, the white man only wants us under the ground because we are a great threat. They think of us as worms, not people. The Great Spirit gave us all the spiritual right to this land and everything we need to live here forever. The white man will take everything that is ours by force — nature and all of our natural belongings. But, he doesn't know the risk that one day everything may be taken from him by nature. Pachamama, Mother Earth, cries tears of pain seeing on her children being massacred and innocent blood covering our soil. I ask you all to have faith in the Great Spirit. Fight! We must defend our land with the bravery of the great warriors and leaders we are, even if victory is not in this world but only in the land of the Great Spirit. We must live or die for what we believe in. We came to this world to serve a mission in life — to be Native Americans. Pachamama, Mother Earth, is our mother, and the Great Spirit is our Father and Creator. If we have to taste the bitter fruit of all that I have said here, then all we are left with is to fight with courage and dignity to the end. If all I have predicted here happens, justice and victory will surely not be in this world nor in our time on earth."

Depressed and with tear-filled eyes, White Wolf thanked all the leaders for coming and, to give them strength at this difficult moment, invited them to participate in the war dance.

Colonel Phillip's Revenge

A few months passed, and Elvira took advantage of her husband Phillip's trip to London and visited some of her friends in Washington. Since he had been attacked and beaten by Colonel Phillip, Utah was sad, overwhelmed, and now distrusted everything and everyone. Racial conflict was getting worse. The captain and his marksmen ruthlessly attacked more indigenous camps with cannons, rifles, and pistols.

The guns left the ground everywhere soaked with Native American blood. The captain was away from home for more than two weeks. Happy with the conquest of the new Dakota Territory, he did not bother to return home, but instead did his usual drunken partying with his friends.

Mother Nature contracted as if it were giving birth to a harsh winter, and with it came a blizzard and the return of Colonel Phillip to Captain Harold's door. He had learnt that the captain was away on a war mission attacking the Sioux Indians. With a pistol in hand, he surreptitiously entered the home. Salish was by the fire when she heard the front door open. She went to see who it was, and her body trembled when she faced Colonel Phillip with a gun pointed at her. Careful to not let anyone hear what was happening, he quietly said, "What kisses those lips could offer me." He waved the gun around Salish's body. She understood his evil intentions and immediately kicked him hard in his genitalia. He responded with a blow that knocked her to the ground, and screamed, "You should make things easier for me, you Indian whore, or I'll have to send you to hell."

"You pathetic white man, I wouldn't dirty my bed with a worm like you. I would rather you kill me, that is if you even have the courage." Salish was beaten and her clothes were ripped as he tried to rape her. Aiyana and Emma heard her cries. Aiyana's Native American blood took over, and to settle things with the colonel, she took a sharp knife from the kitchen. But when she saw it, she did not believe her eyes — a wild animal was forcefully holding an innocent mestiza. Aiyana held the long, sharp knife tightly and fearlessly, and pointed it at the colonel who laughed when he saw the warrior woman.

"Now, I'll really leave here happy. I have to kill one more of you creatures." Aiyana held the sharp knife firmly, knocked the gun from his hand, and kicked it away and far from Salish.

She fought with the colonel. As the matriarch of the Cherokee tribe, Aiyana had received valuable lessons from White Wolf about how to defend herself from the white man with the powerful 'wolf dance of avoidance'. Seeing his grandmother in mortal danger and hearing horses approaching, Utah ran out of the house screaming for help. His cries were heard by the three approaching men, who were apparently drunk! It was the captain returning, accompanied by two other soldiers.

Surprised, Captain Harold asked Utah, "What's going on? I barely get home and I am met with screams. Where is Salish?" Utah was now trembling with fear. "Sir, your wife is in danger in your house."

The captain sobered up rather quickly and ran into the house with the two other soldiers. There, they found the sad scene. Salish's clothes were ripped, and she was on the floor, unconscious and she looked like she was dead. As a great warrior of Mother Earth, Aiyana defended her indigenous sister and injured and disarmed the colonel. She had stabbed him in his arm, but was now suffering his kicks.

The captain realized what had happened, and the soldiers recognized the colonel. Fearing the consequences of what they saw, the two soldiers fled in terror for fear of reprisals from the colonel. Nobody saw anything! The captain, now well 'sobered up', led the colonel to his study.

"I cannot believe you came here trying to take another man's wife, trying to rape her, you animal! I knew you were no good, but with my wife! You, my daughter's husband!

If you don't leave here right now, I will report you for breaking a recent Military Alliance. I heard from my contacts in the Dakota Territory that you sent false reports and broke Peace Treaties with the Indians, causing many deaths with the intention of turning the Generals against the Governor and getting into political office yourself."

With an open wound in his arm and blood dripping everywhere, the colonel was dizzy, upset, and surprised by the captain's sudden arrival and the unexpected retaliation. Colonel Phillip left, embarrassed by the injury that the Native American woman had given him, a worm crawling out of the house, never to return again.

Even though he was somewhat drunk, the captain dealt with the situation very well. He thanked Aiyana for saving Salish's life.

At that moment, he thought, *It was not by chance that I brought this warrior back home with me. She's worth more to me than a soldier on my doorstep.* He called Emma, who had fearfully locked herself in a back room.

"Emma, get out of there and take care of the wounded. The devil has servants like you in droves!"

After all this commotion, White Moon was now awakened. When she didn't see anyone, she called for Aiyana. Even in pain and wounded, she went to care for the dear child. The captain, who was near White Moon's room by chance, was surprised hearing the conversation. "Grandma Aiyana, who is the strong and handsome Indian that always comes to see me? He sings a beautiful song for me to go to sleep almost every night."

Aiyana was so pleased by what she had heard that she bowed and thanked the Great Spirit that White Moon was safe and that she was being taken care of. "My dear child, at the right time I will tell you who he is," she responded. The little girl spoke in Cherokee and English as Salish and Aiyana had taught her.

White Moon was already having conflicts with the captain and White Wolf, without really knowing who they were in her life.

After hearing these words, the captain didn't have the courage to go up to the girl and kiss her, but he thought, *It's time to attack White Wolf. He really is a clever mystic. If he really can appear to Samira in a dream, then through her I can find out where he has hidden the gold in the Cherokee Territory.*

White Wolf's Rescue Mission

A few months passed, and the Cherokee chief feared defeat. The other chiefs didn't listen to his advice and were divided. They didn't know how to negotiate with the white man. They believed in vain promises and mistrusted and betrayed each other. There was, unfortunately, complete chaos on both sides. To White Wolf's dismay, he heard that the indigenous nations were mistreating the American soil. He could not interfere in the spiritual or physical destiny of his tribe, much less that of the others.

One day, with these sorrowful thoughts, White Wolf breathed in the fresh mountain air, witnessing the freedom of the birds, and with them his thoughts also took flight. *"Tonight, I'm going to meet White Moon and Aiyana. I have to rescue my daughter because she is the only one that gives me the courage to live. If I don't, I will make my brother Amitola the chief."*

The warrior concentrated, took the pipe, and asked not to be interrupted by anyone. He thoughtfully walked into his tent. He dedicated the night to the Great Spirit. All he wanted was to visit his daughter in her dreams, even if he had to turn over the yellow metal. To have his daughter back, he was willing to selflessly give away any wealth held in the Cherokee territory.

"Supernatural happenings" occurred that night when the sky celebrated the arrival of the full moon and the hope of spiritual communication of love and happiness between hungry souls.

White Moon was in a deep sleep when suddenly she dreamt that her delicate feet were walking on luscious green grass, approaching a small stream. A violet rainbow on a pink cloud brought Morning Flower to the right, and next to her, on a blue cloud, was chief White Wolf, happy and content to see Morning Flower and his daughter.

The rainbow shone white light on the little girl's path, and from the small stream, an angel of golden light, with large, delicate wings, a white robe down to her feet, and surrounded by a golden light, and an angel emerged. Her eyes, indigo blue, looked like two stars, emitting a bright light that was hard to distinguish from the stars in the sky.

The angel moved towards White Moon, overhead in the air. Surrounded by rays of silver, Aiyana, the matriarch, appeared, following a lighted path, which showed the Great Spirit's divine wisdom. She picked up the little girl and took her to Morning Flower's arms.

"Morning Flower, seize this new opportunity that life has given you to enjoy what has come from your womb, daughter of the earth!" the Guardian Angel of Life softly whispered. "White Moon," she continued, "I present to you your Father and Mother, Children of the Heavens and Inheritors of the Earth." With all the love in her heart, Morning Flower cherished the girl, kissing her rosy face and beautiful braids.

Then appeared White Wolf, and confused by the appearance of the Guardian Angel, who was sent by the Great Spirit, he kissed the angel's hands of light with great respect and asked, "Where do you belong in the sky? Are you for the white man or have you adopted the colored feathers of the indigenous nations as well?"

"My warrior," the angel answered, "I belong to the Light. I am the Guardian Angel of the white man, the Native American, and all the Nations on the Earth. There will be a day that the Great Spirit will make everyone understand that they are all one, without divisions of race, color, or material wealth. Earth Warrior, you are an instrument of the Divine love of God. The Great Spirit of the Native Americans is God to the white man. I want you to know that I'm glad you will give up the yellow metal to have your daughter back. She is now yours and free in your dreams so that you enjoy all the love that the white man has taken from you."

The father, mother, daughter, and sister — finally together — reveled in an embrace. The Guardian Angel, to seal and celebrate the heartfelt union, drew a ring with golden rays around them. White Moon, as if she had already had this dream, happily and naturally called them father and mother. At that moment, the girl did not remember anything about earth, much less the captain. The Guardian Angel had planted the seed of truth in White Moon's heart.

The happiness of that unique moment was interrupted when the Angel of Light pointed again to the sky, toward a large clock marking their return to earth. Morning Flower kissed the warrior's face and hugged him tightly. "I'll wait for you, warrior of my heart. Keep faithful to your tribal principles and protect our daughter, because she will need it," she said. With these last words, Morning Flower was taken away by the pink cloud.

White Wolf understood the message well. He pleaded with great sadness and all the strength in his heart. "Morning Flower, after so long, don't go away. I will continue waiting until the day the Great Spirit unites us again." White Moon felt her father's heart saddened by the departure of her mother, and, with the purity of a child's heart, she quietly whispered, "My father, don't cry. The Great Spirit will bring her back."

"Yes, I know," White Wolf replied. He went toward his sister and embraced her affectionately. He knew that she was not there by chance. He pleaded, "Aiyana! My earth and heart sister, as a witness of the Divine Will of the Great Spirit, pay close attention! Tell the white man that I want to meet him at the next waning moon in a cave near the Smoky Mountain before sunset. I'll tell him where I hide the yellow metal, and in return I want White Moon back." Aiyana, aware of everything she had witnessed, nodded. She knew she had a new mission. Hearing the warrior's last words, White Moon was carried on the Guardian Angel's lap back to her home. White Wolf, radiant with happiness for the opportunity to see his beloved daughter, Morning Flower, and his sister again, returned to his tent. White Moon woke up very happy and immediately called Aiyana to tell her about the dream she had about meeting her Native American father and mother.

Aiyana then went to Utah's room to tell him everything that happened during that magical night.

Emma had prepared pancakes, syrup, apple pie, and strong coffee. To the captain's surprise, White Moon was up early and already sitting on her seat at the table when he arrived. "Samira, why do you have such a large grin on your face so early?" he asked her. "Father, an angel with white wings brought me to meet my new father, White Wolf, and my mother Morning Flower." The captain, who was savoring his coffee, gasped at what he just heard.

"You saw what?" Shocked, the captain called for Salish. "Samira has had a nightmare. The dead do not come back after they have been buried." Salish was stunned. She picked up some toys for White Moon and led her to the orchard to play outside the house.

Captain Harold's blood was boiling and he lost his composure and had a fit of rage. He shouted for Aiyana, who did not understand what he said. "Aiyana, explain to me what you had to do with what Samira just said."

She looked him in the face and replied, "Mapiya" ("this is meant to happen").

Emma, hearing the whole thing, asked Utah to translate it in English for them. "Sir, Aiyana said that Samira saw the Great Spirit of God, and Aiyana told me everything that happened with Samira, who is called White Moon by Cherokees. White Wolf has a message for you, Sir. At the next waning moon, he has arranged a meeting in the cave near the Rocky Mountains. He asked you to take White Moon. If all goes as promised, White Moon will be returned and he will reveal to you where the yellow metal can be found in the Cherokee territory."

The captain laughed, but after considering it, he raised his arms and said, "Utah, tell her that I will do as the chief asked. Now go away!"

I have to admit that this Shaman is really bold, he thought, I will go armed and prepare an ambush. None of White Wolf's powers will be able to save his life now.

Salish had heard everything that Utah said through the back door. She was very frightened and thought it best to keep quiet and pretend to know nothing. At the right time, she would talk to Aiyana. But her thoughts were interrupted by the sound of horses' hooves, announcing Elvira's arrival. Salish felt her heart sink again. She took a deep breath and prayed. "Great Spirit, protect White Moon from the treacherous hands of this enemy and the captain's ambitions."

Salish was interrupted by Elvira's arrival. "Where are the servants in this house?" she shouted. "Salish, don't just stare at me like some stupid fly. Didn't my father teach you your duties? Wait on me now. Get my bags with Utah. I am very tired." Salish put her head down and did what she was told. The captain was in the living room, admiring his collection of weapons. Which one would he select to kill the chief, make him disappear, and find out where the gold was hidden? Now that she knew the truth through her dream, he didn't want any competition between White Wolf and him for his daughter's heart.

Elvira barged in. "Who will be your next victim of war? I want you to know that the beating Aiyana gave my husband has cost me very dearly — separation and soon divorce!"

"I am not scared of Colonel Phillip. He has no decency with his attempted rape. If it weren't for you, I would have used one of these guns to blow out the brains of your unfaithful husband," said her father.

"Her accusation doesn't stand up. Between his word and that of your half-breed Indian, he wins."

The captain was now very angry and shouted, "Elvira, by any chance, did the colonel make midnight confessions to you to believe him over your own father? I don't want you to bring any more dirt into my house. Let's get to the point! At the next waning moon, I'll meet with the chief of the Cherokee tribe, the father of White Moon, my Samira. Unfortunately, I run the risk of him taking the girl. The objective is to find out where the gold is hidden and then return Samira to White Wolf." Elvira's eyes widened with admiration, and she said, "You have a beautiful golden card up your sleeve, an illegitimate Indian daughter to get the Cherokees' gold."

"Don't ridicule me. Help me with solutions."

Elvira ran her fingers over one of captain's guns and revealed her cruel plan.

"I have thought of a way to send the Cherokee chief to hell and keep both the gold and Samira. Of course, I will only tell you if you share all your information with me."

"Spit it out!" he said, angry again. "Your grotesque ways irritate me."

"It is very simple," she replied. "Colonel Phillip has a war tactic that always works when the enemy doesn't deliver the information to pass on the location of the yellow metal. A few times a year, he sends for scorpions to be brought from Mexico. With just one sting, they do the job, the enemy with terrible pain will deliver the information, and live for few days without anyone having to do it and get blood on their hands."

"In this case, I don't want to use my weapons on White Wolf in front of Samira."

"Since when is your love for this little Indian girl greater than that you have for me? I have spent many years of my life watching you commit massacres," Elvira replied.

"Rest assured, dear father!" she added, "I will get the scorpions in a tightly sealed box by the next waning moon and leave them for you in your gun cabinet. Don't forget to lock it, or some curious person will find certain death!"

Elvira, humming to herself, left the house. She did not have the sensitivity to feel any remorse for the horror she had concocted. Aiyana, passing her as she came in, was shocked at the dark spirits and the aura all around Elvira.

Something very bad was about to happen, she realized. She went to Salish's bedroom and told her what she had seen around Elvira.

For a few days, as they waited for the arrival of the waning moon, everything was quiet. Mother Nature shrank to protect the earth from the impending attack of evil. As promised, Elvira sent the Mexican scorpions to her father. Cold and calculating, he took the box the day before the meeting and let the deadly creatures out in the cave.

When White Moon woke up, she was very upset as she also sensed that something very bad was going to happen. "My Indian princess, I noticed that you have not eaten. Soon we will leave on a trip. If you are good and do what I say, I will do anything you want," the captain said. But she did not want to eat. And the sad girl, without knowing what was going to happen, ran into his arms.

Salish, suspicious of Elvira and her husband, stayed vigilant. The captain began to call out orders. "Get our daughter ready and dress her warmly. I'll leave soon and go far from here along with Utah. I have a mission."

"What are you talking about?" Salish asked him. "Our daughter will not leave here without me."

Furious, the captain shouted, "Don't make me hurt you. Get out of my way, Salish. This is none of your business. Do what I asked you to do and get our daughter ready. Don't make me mad. My blood is boiling because I have something important to do, and I need you to be quiet. I promise that I'll bring Samira back to the house."

Aiyana restlessly walked from one side of the house to the other, knowing that the inevitable would happen. She asked Utah to accompany White Moon and help her if she needed it. Utah left the house, the wind was blowing hard, and he took courage from this and went to talk to the captain.

"Captain! Excuse me if I am interfering where I shouldn't be. Aiyana asked for permission to accompany White Moon if she needs it. I can't handle a crying child like her alone."

Captain Harold's eyes widened at his boldness.

"Stop right there. Sometimes I forget that you are an Indian. Where do you get your boldness from? Maybe it is your contact with the white man that lets you play both sides. You are like a monkey that runs when there is a problem and then returns with the solution. Very well, tell Aiyana that she can accompany us to look after the child. If there is a snake there, she will be worth something to me. What I admire most about you is your cleverness and courage to face me."

The captain, controlling the wagon, led the way to the cave.

It was windy and cold. They travelled for hours. White Moon slept on Aiyana's warm lap, Utah was unsure and worried about everyone's safety, and the captain had a worried look on his face throughout. The route was dangerous and full of surprises.

Suddenly, as the captain whipped the horses to go a little faster, they encountered a herd of wild buffaloes that were beginning to cross the road. He quickly took the rifle and fired several times at the buffaloes, killing a few and starting a stampede. Scared by the shots, White Moon awoke. Once all the buffaloes had passed, Captain Harold spotted the fateful cave.

As soon as they got there, Harold told Utah to tell Aiyana to take care of Samira and stay in the wagon until he gave further orders.

Utah was shaking with fear, not knowing what was going to happen. "Now, I want to see your courage," the captain told Utah, "Go to the cave and call for White Wolf and tell him that the time has come! Tell me everything he says as I don't understand his language." Utah went ahead, and the captain followed behind him.

But before Utah entered the cave, White Wolf felt the presence of his daughter and sister and emerged to meet the captain. Surprised on seeing White Wolf well, the captain said, "I am amazed you are healthy, with the scorpions in the cave! What powers are you using?"

With a steady gaze, and like a hungry lion about to eat, White Wolf stared into the captain's eyes, ignoring his comments, having disposed of the scorpions. "Utah," he said, "tell the white man that I left fear in my mother's womb. I will tell him where the yellow metal is after seeing my daughter and Aiyana. I can feel their presence very close to me. Where are they?"

Utah translated the message.

"White Wolf, I'll only let your daughter and sister get out of the wagon if you promise me that you will not use any of your witchcraft and show me where the gold is hidden in the Cherokee territory."

Utah tried to translate everything that the captain said. His hands and face were covered in cold sweat. It was unsafe for his beloved White Moon. How would he protect her from the hands of that heartless white man, who pretended to be her father to take advantage of the chief? His heart was heavy, but his thoughts were interrupted when the captain shouted, "Hurry up! It is not the time for you to have your head in the clouds. Tell him if he goes near the wagon — unarmed of course — I will have Aiyana and White Moon come down." Thrilled, the warrior approached the wagon. The child's eyes were full of tears and her heart pounded with emotion. She got down, running into White Wolf's arms, who was now lost in another dimension of happiness, when the captain interrupted him. White Wolf felt the captain's gun touch his stomach.

"No witchcraft!" the captain shouted. "If you want to see your daughter again, just tell me where the gold is hidden." Utah could not bring himself to translate the captain's last words, and the captain slapped him hard. So, Utah obeyed the order and translated. For a moment, White Wolf feared the worst for his daughter and humbly bowed his head. Picking up a small branch, he drew several lines in the ground where the trail started and where the gold was hidden in the Cherokee territory. But the captain suspected that he was not telling the truth. "This can't be right," he shouted! "The US Army has searched this area for quite some time and nothing was found here!" White Wolf was underestimating his intelligence. The captain thought fast. *What if he's buying time to do some 'trick', kill me, and take Samira away from me? I can't take this risk.* He shouted in despair, "Utah, tell White Wolf I do not believe that this is the right place. If he doesn't tell me the truth, I will arrest him and turn him over to the US Military, and he will be hung for lying. The choice is his."

White Wolf continued to draw in the sand with the branch as before, adding even more information about where the gold was hidden. Before he could finish, someone hidden behind a large bush, appeared behind him. "Sensing movement behind him, the chief turned. A long-barreled weapon appeared and fired at him, hitting him right at his heart."

The Shaman's back was soon drenched in blood, and he fell to the ground with his eyes fixed on White Moon. This was the last breath of the Cherokee chief.

The captain, astonished, stood motionless, his eyes bulging. From behind the foliage of the leafy bush, emerged Elvira, wearing a US soldier's uniform that she had stolen from her father. In her hand, she held a rifle — the captain's favorite weapon — that could only turn out be the curse of destiny.

Aiyana felt her heart cut by pain, realizing that her brother would now never be able to live with White Moon, his daughter. She concluded to herself: My brother died for love. The white woman was a traitor. She used the powerful weapon. She sensed White Moon's complete desperation and taking her shawl, covered and comforted the girl so she would not have to witness this sad ending any further, and led her to the wagon.

"I wanted to kill him with my own hands," Elvira said. "His Indian daughter is no better than me. I wanted to make it clear to you and the Cherokees from now on who is in charge. Now, with White Wolf's map, I will command the withdrawal of the gold from the Cherokee territory."

The captain, his fists clenched, screamed, "Where the hell did you come from, you idiot, and who told you to come here? What if, as he has indicated, this is not the right place where the gold is hidden?"

"Maybe it is not right, but the trail exists," Elvira said. "Living with your husband and his bad company has made you stupid. I wanted White Wolf alive to turn into the army. What does he do for me dead? What side of the military are you on? It seems like you are willing to trade information with other US Army Generals." To this, Elvira gave a fake and challenging smile.

"All in good time, father. Don't worry about the body. I will throw it off the nearest cliff myself. I don't want the Shaman's ghost haunting me."

Utah, reeling and trembling from all he had just witnessed, joined Aiyana. The captain now realized that Elvira was much worse than he had imagined, and for the first time, he was startled by her wickedness and evil. The information he had obtained was now in the hands of his daughter as well." He climbed back on the wagon and whipped the horses to leave quickly, returning home by the light of the full moon. Mother Nature was filled with pain from the loss of one of the Shamans of the earth — a true warrior! His only desire was to have the right to raise his only surviving daughter, who was now in the hands of the white man, torn between two cultures.

Elvira stayed around the area for a while. She brutally wounded one of the legs of the warrior's white horse when it stopped her from throwing White Wolf's body over a cliff.

Hours later, the chief's brother, descending from the mountains with other Native Americans, saw White Wolf's now lame horse coming toward them, completely out of control. To everyone's surprise, the Shaman's favorite horse fell dead to the ground right in front of them!

Amitola let out a great painful cry that was heard throughout the mountains. "It can't be! He has come to tell us. I feel that my brother is dead. Quickly! Come on!" With uncertainty in their hearts, they left to follow the horse's trail.

A great eagle accompanied and guided them to the site where White Wolf died. When Amitola realized that his brother was shot, drenched in blood, he felt a glow of love and acceptance in his eyes. His heart heavy with mourning after shedding many tears, Amitola — the new leader of the Cherokees — put his brother's on his horse and headed for his high Rocky Mountains. They were accompanied by the great eagle, proving to his brother and other warriors that White Wolf was, even in death, a faithful son of the earth.

Once they arrived at the camp, the news got around soon, and the sounds of weeping and wailing were heard from the entire tribe. They gathered in a circle and prepared White Wolf to be buried with a ceremony to honor the Great Spirit and Mother Earth.

The Allies of Betrayal

Elvira was not pleased to have abandoned the body of White Wolf and his fatally wounded horse. To avoid further friction with her father, she whipped her horse and went quickly to a nearby town to see Colonel Phillip. Hours later, she arrived at her home and was surprised to see one of the soldiers from the colonel's regiment carrying all her husband's bags to a military wagon. She slowly entered the house.

"Why did you come back?" the colonel screamed. "What hellish battle have you been in with that bloody army clothing? Where did you get that army uniform? I was hoping you had understood that our marriage ended some time ago. Unfortunately, I have to see you again in this sad situation. You remind me of one of my soldiers."

"Don't go away! I have something that would be of interest to you," Elvira replied. "If not, I will sell this secret to another American colonel. Take it or leave it!"

"In that case, we'll go to my office," he responded. "I don't want anyone listening to us."

Elvira, even though she was unassuming as a woman, was very sly and cunning as a fox. She knew how to manipulate and feed the colonel's ambitions. She walked to the bedroom and took a large diamond out of the safe. She faltered for a moment, contemplating whether she should share the secret with her husband. On the other hand, she imagined no longer being at the side of a powerful man like Phillips, a man who also has political access.

"Come here right away, woman! There is no time to lose," her husband cried.

She went to the office and quietly said, "I have a proposal for you. I will only be your ally if you stop this divorce and come live with me again. I have had this large diamond in this safe that I stole from my father. It belongs to Samira, White Moon, his adopted daughter, and heiress to all the Cherokee gold."

"What do you want?" the colonel asked, his eyes fixed on the diamond. He came closer and took the diamond from Elvira's hand. It glittered and glinted with a bright sparkle. He could hardly believe his eyes.

"Well, let's negotiate!"

Elvira extended her hand. "If you say yes, here's the map to the trail of gold."

He was analyzing the facets of the diamond. "I have to admit that this is one of the most stunning and largest gems that I have ever seen. I will arrange to have the divorce cancelled."

Elvira raised her voice, taking command of the situation. "I want half the Cherokee gold," she said. "I must admit that the way you negotiate in situations of power scares me," he said, surprised. "I will very carefully prepare a military plan to remove the gold at the right time. The biggest problem will be your father — the enemy."

"My father didn't even realize that I stole this diamond out of his locked safe along with the rifle that killed White Wolf and sent him to hell," Elvira shamelessly replied.

"How did you find out about the treasure?" the colonel asked with admiration.

"My father told me the whole truth," Elvira replied coldly, "When I pretended to be against you, of course, he trusted me. As far as the diamond is concerned, I just happened to walk into the room and heard Salish tell Emma the whole story of White Moon's birth."

The colonel laughed, amazed at his wife's intelligence. "Elvira, my beloved. Did you betray your father out of jealousy because of Salish and me?" Elvira widened her blue eyes and protested.

"Go to hell. You can see things the way you want. In life, the one with the best cards on the table wins. I am going to go to the bathroom to take off these bloodstained clothes, and with the new lavender I brought from London, I will become an exciting new woman. I want to have your kisses. My father's mixed-blood woman would be jealous if she saw my new wardrobe from London."

"Elvira, stop this nonsense! I want to see if you can stop being so bitter and be as good as your word."

Salish Confronts Captain Harold

Things were not going well at captain Harold's home since the death of White Wolf. The robbery of the diamond from the office and Elvira's disappearance left the captain very upset. White Moon was not the same little girl either. Her vibrant and piercing eyes were losing their brightness. Salish did everything to ease her pain and heartache after she learnt what happened.

Aiyana remained silent and avoided the captain. She cried out for help to the Great Spirit. She could not take White Moon from Salish's hands to her tribe without the spiritual approval of the Great Spirit.

The captain learnt from a sergeant from his regiment that his daughter had betrayed him. He said that he had seen her with Colonel Phillip at a social gathering in North Carolina. Now, he had to face two powerful enemies.

Salish was worried and said, "I don't know what to do with Samira. After seeing White Wolf die in front of her, she does not eat well. Her little fingers and little body are getting thinner by the day."

"What do you want me to do?" the captain responded, obviously upset. "She doesn't even want to touch me when I get close. It seems like I have lost Samira's love — along with the diamond that Elvira stole from my safe."

"You are an arrogant and blind man, wake up!" she screamed at him. "Samira is a living diamond. You and your daughter are the only ones responsible for this loss and the hardening of White Moon's heart, which will bleed for the rest of her life. Thanks to the Great Spirit, he made me half Indian, and so I can see the things of the soul that white people just do not see."

"You think you are better than me? Why? Because everyone sees you as an aberration, with your emerald green eyes. You're not an Indian or a white woman," he said, enraged.

"I am what I am!" Salish replied with tears in her eyes. "The Great Spirit made me this way. No matter how I look, it is what's inside of me that is important. There will be a time when I will redeem my half-white self and be at peace, when I can prove to myself that the two halves are the same spiritual identity. Prejudice against Indians does not come from earth; we are her children and also of all the white people who live here."

The captain rose from his chair, and looking surprised, stared at her shouting. "It seems that living with that old warrior has made your native ancestry flourish and you have created an indigenous alliance. What is happening in this house anyway? Salish, you have no respect for me. How can you insult me like that? Go to your room and wait for me there."

"Captain," she replied, "your strong arm does not scare me as it did before. I will not stop speaking the truth and what I feel in my heart."

The captain did not understand this change in his wife. "Get away from me, you sassy and ungrateful Indian. What was I thinking of, getting involved with a mixed Indian?"

He was tempted to be violent with Salish. He thought about everything he heard and went to talk to Utah.

"Utah, let Aiyana know that I do not want her to talk with Salish anymore. My wife is already speaking the native Cherokee language. Her job is to take care of this house and Samira. Nothing else. Understood? If I see her talking to Salish, I will take her to an Indian reservation myself. One that is guarded by officers that gives daily beatings if you do not obey." Utah was perplexed with this reprimand and went to tell Aiyana about it.

Utah and Aiyana knew that things were getting very complicated for both of them.

A few months passed. Snow fell, covering the earth with a soft, white covering. White Moon was very cold and had to always rub her hands together. She fell asleep quickly and was 'spiritually transported' to the mountains where her Cherokee tribe lived. She saw her people sheltered in buffalo and antelope hides and with decorated and colorful blankets. White Wolf approached her and gave her a tight hug. The little girl cried!

"E do da," the little girl cried ("father" in Cherokee).

"Good! I see that Aiyana taught you your first words in our native language," said the Shaman.

The girl, with a very happy smile, replied, "Yes, and I want to stay here with you. Please don't leave me. I don't want to stay with Daddy Harold. He is evil and hits my mother Salish. Where is "e tsi", my mother?" When she heard the request, Morning Flower stepped out of a pink-colored cloud.

"Daughter, my heart is broken by the pain. I'm here! Don't fear Captain Harold. You will get away from him with the help of Salish, your adoptive mother, and Aiyana. The two of them together will know how to lead you to your new life cycle on earth. The Great Spirit will make it so."

White Moon, without understanding everything her mother said, took some daisies that were around her neck and gave them as a gift of love. The Shaman was holding a beautiful dove, white as snow, which he gave to his daughter.

"White Moon, be obedient to your indigenous family," he said. "We will always be here. Aiyana will teach you the spiritual teachings of Mother Earth, Pachamama. May the Great Spirit always protect and comfort you."

The sweet girl woke up crying and calling out for "e do da" and "e tsi".

Captain Harold Ambushed

There was a big dispute between Elvira and her husband for the Cherokees gold. The rumor of its existence was discussed in many social circles of the United States. To get to the trail map drawn by White Wolf, and since it was also in the hands of Captain Harold, Colonel Phillip would have to be cunning. The captain was well aware of the colonel's trickery and underhanded tactics.

The colonel was scheduled to meet with an 'Army General War Council' to discuss new attacks on other indigenous nations because the Native Americans were considered incapable of owning land — the white man trying to hide his lust for gold and territorial ambition behind the incapability of the indigenous people.

A few sad and turbulent months for the indigenous nations passed. Mother Nature witnessed more violence and massacres.

One day, after yet another bloody battle with the Sioux tribe, Captain Harold and his regiment were returning by moonlight.

On a narrow road that cut through some large rocks, he heard a wolf howl.

Even though he was amongst many soldiers, with many others in command, he was jolted when a shower of arrows came from Native Americans who were well hidden in the trees. Then an arrow hit the captain in the back. The ambush was quite unexpected.

He lost his balance and fell from his horse. Even though he was weakened and without energy, he screamed, "Take your positions! Fire! Kill them all!"

During the shootout, the Sioux Indians and the US soldiers fought fiercely. In the chaos that followed, the horses trampled over Captain Harold, who was lying on the road. His eyes open, he bled to death — a sad ending for his life's journey. The peace treaty between the Sioux Indians and the US Government was broken. When the Native Americans withdrew, the soldiers took the captain's body to the fort. Both sides sustained many casualties.

A New Life for White Moon

Elvira and Colonel Phillip, who both plotted and allied with evil, received the news together. The colonel faked a forced look of sadness and grief for his 'enemy'. As if taken over by grief and pain, he put his hand over his heart and said, "Elvira, my dear, unfortunately, like the colonel, I couldn't do anything. The Sioux Indian attack was a complete surprise. I don't know where they came from."

"I appreciate your concern," Elvira said. "Yes, I understand. Even with the military and social differences between you and my father, I believe it was fate." She threw her arms around her husband, asking for his help to cope with the death of her father. Her words were like honey for the colonel's mind. He had been warned that the area — where the captain was killed — was vulnerable to Sioux attacks. Thus, it was easy to sabotage the military intelligence and eliminate his archenemy.

The sound of approaching horses interrupted the colonel's thoughts. It was Salish, wearing colorful Native American clothing and demonstrating her new indigenous identity. She was accompanied by Utah, and she was calling for Elvira. "Phillip, come quickly," Elvira called her husband. "I must be dreaming."

"What brings you here?" Elvira mockingly asked Salish.

Inside, Salish faced Elvira, the shrew. "This morning, a military officer told me about my husband's death. When he learned of White Moon, he made it clear that I will lose her because I am a mestiza. As you know, it was a penance to live with your father due to our racial difference, but it's still a loss and I'm not made of stone. Elvira, after you bury your father, give me the opportunity to raise White Moon, as your father would have wished."

The colonel interrupted Salish. "Ah! I can see that the Indian has come out of hiding. Now without the support of her husband — she will probably starve! As for Samira, the heiress of the Cherokees, I want to make it clear that the US Social Services, and not some Tribal Council, will decide what should be done with her."

"Get out of our house!" Elvira backed her husband. "Your racial situation is so complicated that I don't know if I should turn you in to an Indian reservation or have you arrested for contempt against the authority of Colonel Phillip. You decide!"

Utah was frightened that Salish would lose her temper with Elvira. He signaled to her that they should leave. At that moment, Salish realized that Utah was right. To go against her two archenemies would not have been prudent. Her green eyes were now more vibrant and filled with tears. Weak and without retaliating against the couple, Salish and Utah went back home.

Once they got home, Utah, the young warrior, with a sinking heart — because of all the lies that were being told — called Salish to tell her that he knew about the captain's death. "Salish, because of the indigenous blood that runs through my veins, I must confess something to you. I heard through the Sioux Indians that the colonel was plotting against them. No one knew the day and or the hour of the attack. The colonel was advised by the army to attack. The Sioux Indians, trying to disarm a booby trap in the forest, captured one of Colonel Phillip's officers. A day before, under torture, he revealed that Colonel Phillip had sent Captain Harold in his place at the behest of another army colonel, and two sergeants were bribed not to warn the captain about the traps in the forest. The Sioux hid every day in the trees, waiting for the colonel and his soldiers. And, instead of Colonel Phillip, your husband was killed."

Salish shuddered at Utah's confession, and breathing fire she screamed, "That damn traitor! He had no right to have Harold killed. I'd rather it had happened at the hands of fate than by his hand. Now I know what to do! I cannot rely on a couple of snakes to protect White Moon."

Salish felt battered and called Aiyana. "We'll pack up all our belongings. Unfortunately, I can't continue with Emma's services. As soon as the sun rises, we will leave to the mountains, where the Cherokee tribe is. With the blessings of the Great Spirit and Mother Earth, that will be our refuge. Aiyana, what do you think?"

"Yes!" the old matriarch answered. It is time for White Moon's new learning cycle of her indigenous roots to begin. Amitola is my brother and he is the new Cherokee chief. When other chiefs unite with Amitola, it will be harder for them to take our Cherokees' inheritance."

They began to organize their main belongings for their departure.It was a very busy night. Emma was very upset by the captain's death. She had also become very attached to Aiyana and little White Moon. Before White Moon awoke, she left the house with a heavy heart and went to her eldest brother's house, the pastor of an Evangelical Church in North Carolina. She left the address for Salish and Aiyana.

The sun with its shining and golden rays rose next morning, and the enchanted full moon returned to its heavenly home.

Aiyana was up early and called Utah "Utah, I don't trust those couple of snakes. They are thieves. We need guns."

"Aiyana, I think you're right. I'll ask for Salish's permission and get one of the captain's weapons."

"Yes!" Aiyana said. "Only use it if it is necessary, and you can hide it under your clothes. I am very worried about them, worried that they will come after us. Also, after all, it is a long and dangerous journey, and there are hazards like wild buffaloes that will cross the road, so we must be careful."

A few hours passed, Aiyana and Utah had put all the belongings in the wagon, and Salish was preparing the horses for the trip. White Moon cried, asking for her Daddy. She wanted to know where he was and why she could not bring all the toys that he used to play with her along. She had not yet told White Moon about the captain's death. She was lost in thought and did not notice the unexpected arrival of Colonel Phillip and Elvira.

Aiyana, who was leading White Moon to the wagon, was surprised and amazed with the intuition that the Great Spirit had revealed about these vipers. Colonel Phillip dismounted and pointed to Salish with a cane he held in his hand.

"Ah, look, we caught that damned Indian leaving the house with the heiress of the Cherokees."

Aiyana gave a steady and discrete look to Utah, urging the use of the gun if he needed to. Salish, her heart in her mouth, cried out.

"Colonel, it seems that our destinies intersect again. I don't owe you anything! Get out of my way! I am the free and proud owner of my destiny."

Elvira had a paper in her hand that was signed by a government agent, asking for temporary custody of Samira. "This is the authorization that Samira belongs to me and my husband until the case goes to trial in the Supreme Court."

Salish immediately took White Moon and shouted, "Elvira, you're a bitter snake. Don't you even dare try to take White Moon from me, or I'll kill you with my own two hands, you viper."

Elvira quickly lunged toward Salish and brutally and forcibly snatched White Moon from her, beating, kicking, and screaming at her. "I knew you were a chicken."

The colonel used his whip on Salish, knocking her to the ground. He took the gun from his belt, put his finger on the trigger, and pointed it at Salish's head.

But Aiyana, like a fierce black panther, with a small knife that she had hidden underneath her tunic, jumped on top of him, throwing the gun far away from him. For the second time, she faced the colonel in a brutal fight. Using her knife, she delivered a sharp blow to the colonel's lungs while Utah slyly took his concealed weapon and pointed it at Elvira. The colonel screamed in pain, unable to move. From the wagon, Aiyana got some rope and tied the two of them to a tree in front of the house.

Utah, after defending his family, asked them to climb on the wagon. The snakes had underestimated them.

He led them into the mountains and except for Salish's occasional moaning in pain, they travelled in silence.

"Salish, be strong," Aiyana consoled her. "I know that your head is hurting you but try to sleep — the journey will be long and difficult. Once we arrive at the village, Amitola will personally take care of your injuries to your body and soul. Don't worry about White Moon, she can sleep on my lap."

White Moon fell asleep on her lap, and in the Divine sleep of the innocence and purity of children, was transported to Heaven.

In the invisible dream world, White Moon found herself walking on emerald green grass. The sun bathed her in rays of white and gold that mingled with the delicate lilacs and the numerous violets in the field. A light violet angel walked in this dimension of life and light. Above her head was a bright blue star, and she was wearing a pearly white robe that reflected white light. Light came through her hands, and she led children of all races of the planet earth. White Moon approached her, and the Guardian Angel of Liberation took her hand and connected her to all the other children, forming a large circle. She and the other children were all different, White Moon realized, but all together in one circle it made no difference. She could, for a moment, see that all the other children and her formed a circle that made up the Earth. With purity and love, the children maintained its energy. And from the sky, a song came, nourishing them with sweet nectar.

The Angel of Liberation went to the center of the circle and praised the Great Spirit. "I proclaim peace and unity amongst all His sons and daughters. The Great Spirit, the giver of life, is at the center of all of their hearts. When He says Amen, everyone will feel the union and there will be no more wars on Planet Earth." With these last words, the Angel of Liberation determined that each child present had a spiritual mission to bring harmony and racial unity amongst all the Great Spirit's sons and daughters on Planet Earth.

After talking with all the children, there was a Spiritual Feast, where sweet fruit was offered to all of them.

White Moon, fed by the Great Spirit, awoke happy. She described everything that happened to Salish and Aiyana in her native Cherokee language.

The Unexpected Arrival

The day dawned and a star that remained in the sky brought hope and peace. After the long journey, Salish recovered after hearing White Moon's whole story with great admiration. Utah was very careful with the horses. When antelopes crossed their path, he controlled the horses and went around them with skill.

Aiyana breathed a sigh of relief and was full of happiness when she saw the High Mountains surrounded by luscious green grass. Colorful birds flew everywhere, giving the feeling of the Divine, and that everything was made by the hand of the Great Spirit.

Utah, by fulfilling his duty, felt happy. "Here we are!" he said, and White Moon jumped off the wagon, tired, but still full of life and went to meet other children who were playing. Amitola was there, and he immediately ran into the arms of his sister, Aiyana. The excitement was so great that both wept with joy at the unexpected reunion. It was the first time Salish had witnessed such a warm encounter of love and friendship. Amitola was surprised to see White Moon. The Cherokee princess wore a white man's dress and was accompanied by a mixed-race woman. With humility and respect, he bowed his head, realizing that this was an opportunity life had given him to learn. He thanked Utah for safely returning his family.

To everyone's surprise, Utah called Aiyana and said, "Dear grandmother, it is with great sadness and heartache that I have made this decision: I cannot live here. It will be easier to help our Cherokee family from the outside because I speak English. My intention is to work with the agents of the American government to help our family from outside the Cherokee territory. Someone from our tribe must live with them and find out about their plans of attack. Grandmother Aiyana, life will be the sweetest for me when I can one day return to take care of White Moon and not be a punching bag for the white man — when I can be respected as a Cherokee. My parents were burned alive in the war, killed by the white man in our Cherokee territory, and so I am asking for your blessing."

Aiyana, emotions running high, with her strong and nurturing arms, hugged Utah. "Let the Great Spirit's Will be done, my beloved son," she said. "I'll always be here, supporting, harboring, and giving strength and courage to our indigenous family. I will not go to the other world without seeing your return here to the mountains."

Salish, also moved by strong emotions, spoke, "Utah, thank you for everything! Come back soon! Take a wagon with horses, and there are still supplies from the trip — and return safely."

The young warrior left, thoughtful and confident that his fate would be different. He would be a messenger and translator for the white man in his dealings with the indigenous nations. With his eyes open to the future, he gave up his freedom to serve a greater calling that life offered him.

Amitola was happy for the return of his sister and niece and prepared a great feast. He presented White Moon to the tribe, who was given a brightly decorated tunic made of animal skins.

A large bonfire was lit, transmitting warmth and tribal union. White Moon, to the surprise and admiration of the other children, made sure that she shared her box full of play things that she had brought with her.

The older women served sweet potatoes and corn in clay utensils. The chest of a buffalo was being roasted. The tribe sang and danced around the sacred fire with their wooden flutes. The crackling sound of the blazing campfire mingled with the notes that were being sung and played for the Great Spirit. Amitola, the chief, asked the elders and his sister to smoke the sacred clay peace pipe. High in the High Mountains, the stars witnessed the return of White Moon and Aiyana to their indigenous roots.

The celebrations lasted all night. Amitola called Aiyana and Salish after everyone had gone to their tents. Anxious about the future of their tribe, the warrior said, "Yesterday, I received sad news from other chiefs about the increasing atrocities against our women and children. The white men are invading the camps with their guns and killing women with babies still in the wombs, disrespecting life, and raping our young virgins. Aiyana, you have been missed greatly by our tribe. You are one of the few women who knows how to defend herself against the white man. Our brother White Wolf sensed that our tribe was not prepared for an attack from the white man against our women. That's why he taught the 'dance of the wolves' defense to you."

After this painful message, Aiyana, who had been sitting on the ground, stood up to speak. "It is my duty to continue my mission to defend my Cherokee sisters. My brother, starting tomorrow,

I ask your permission to start teaching other neighboring villages. I will train Salish, who was nearly killed by the white man twice."

Though she was surprised, Salish fully understood, and her voice was full of emotion. "I need to repay the help I have received from Aiyana. I will learn and teach women to defend their honor from the white man. I ask you to please let me stay with White Moon. I want her by my side."

The matriarch, happy with this union, said, "I thank the Great Spirit for my return to my native people. With faith and hope, I will prepare the women to defend themselves with spears, bows and arrows, and knives."

"Through my union with Aiyana and White Moon, the strength of the forest has been created to defend indigenous women," Salish said, with a happy smile.

There was nothing more to say. Amitola felt the guiding hand of the Great Spirit illuminating and guiding his path. After the ceremony and meeting, everyone was very tired and went back to their tents.

Salish Takes on the Cherokees' Cause

Elvira and Colonel Philip were tied up for a long time until they were finally freed by the colonel's soldiers, who had arrived with news of fresh attacks and riots in indigenous territories." The colonel and Elvira were taken to a military hospital. All they, the vicious couple, wanted was to get their hands on the gold and their revenge against Aiyana and Salish.

God's time was in charge of resolving this racial debt between the couple and the Native Americans.

At the mountains, after a few months of training, Salish could defend herself very well in any situation. She and Aiyana visited other camps, teaching self-defense, spreading love and friendship.

Amitola called Salish for a personal meeting. She was anxious about her new position in the indigenous community and feared that some would not accept her help because of her white ancestry. The cold wind blew strong from the mountains towards her, giving her a clear mind. She was trying to understand the situation. Amitola touched her shoulder and said, "Salish, by living with our tribe, you have regained your indigenous roots. I have something very important for you to do." He brought her to where the gold was. Salish was reminded of the times when she was thrown out of Captain Harold's office when he was alone, contemplating and admiring the piece of gold he had stolen. She was there, she thought, with all the freedom to see what the white man had kept. Now, she was surprised at what she saw.

"For us, it has no value. But our lives are being threatened due to this yellow metal. We need horses. Our supplies will eventually run out and daily hunting and fishing may not be enough to sustain the entire tribe." He took a large piece of gold and continued speaking. "Negotiate with this yellow metal, with the white man. I want you to trade it for horses, guns, and ammunition. Without weapons, it will be difficult to defend ourselves against the white man. Don't reveal who you are."

Salish had sometimes visited European traders with the captain, and they did not realize that she was a mestiza. She spoke English like a white woman, and there were European immigrants everywhere. Together, Amitola and Salish made a plan, to trade the gold in exchange for fast horses and supplies for the tribe.

"It was not by chance that I am here," Salish said, relieved. "Only now do I understand what I felt when the wind was blowing in my direction. It was a sign from the Great Spirit. I have to start moving to bring resources to our tribe."

Salish put her plan into action.

Before the sun rose, Salish dressed herself in an elegant white dress and travelled across the vast plains. When she arrived in the town with the large Trading Post, she passed a young army soldier.

He introduced himself with a bright smile.

"What is a beautiful woman doing in a dreadful place like this?" he asked, not realizing that she was a mestizo, as she looked European.

"I would like to talk to you privately," she said.

Salish invited the soldier to chat near the bushes where she had left the wagon, a good way from the Trading Post.

"I don't want you to misunderstand the situation," she said to the soldier named Eric. He looked a bit shocked.

"I have a business proposition for you," she said. "I want you to pose as my husband to the European Traders. I need horses, military guns, and ammunition, and after this, you can escort me to near the Rocky Mountains. If you accept this, I will give you some nuggets of gold. That's the deal – take it or leave it!"

"Before I decide, show me the gold first," Eric replied, still in shock.

Salish climbed into the wagon and returned with a few nuggets of gold.

Eric's eyes lit up "So you have the gold! I would be rich with this and could buy my way out of the army – and get away from the bloody battle with the Indians!"

"When the delivery is made," Salish said, "you will get your gold."

Eric was very happy with this. He couldn't wait to get the Trading Post with Salish and complete the deal.

Salish, having completed this deal with Eric, went back on her own to the Trading Post and bought more horses, guns, and ammunition.

The Cherokees, thanks to Salish, became well-armed to protect themselves. A great deal of time passed, and they were attacked many times. No one could understand how they had obtained their weapons, and the white man did not dare to go near to the High Mountains area where they lived. However, even with their new weapons, Amitola sensed that something bad was about to happen.

Elvira Ends The Cherokees' String Of Luck

Colonel Phillip was transferred to another state to fight against other indigenous nations. The military focus was far away from the Cherokees — but for a few years. Then there was shocking news. Elvira sold the information about the trail of gold in the Cherokee territory to the US Government.

Colonel Phillip arrived home, furious. His military uniform smelling of gunpowder, and in his big boots, he paced aggressively across the wooden floor. Elvira pretended not to know what had upset him so much!

"I'm in the right mood to slap you across your face, you traitor! My only ally is a snake! How could you betray me and sell that information to the government?"

"Your words do not scare me or intimidate me," Elvira said, staring her husband right in the face. "The tables have turned. I got tired of waiting for a life of luxury in London.

I am not prepared to live any longer with these simple things that you give me. I have had enough of a rough existence. I will now go and be in English high society. Your promises to come back and get our hands on the gold never happened. It was worth it and I'm satisfied. From now on, I will be more respected with the small fortune I have accumulated by selling this information to the government."

The colonel was furious now. Scared of being attacked by him, the colonel's cat had fled and hidden itself behind a long red curtain in the main meeting room. As approached Elvira with a clenched fist to punch her in the face, the cat ran out and jumped at the colonel. Startled, he fell backwards, knocking over a rifle with a bayonet attached, which was in his collection. It pierced his back and entered his lungs — which were previously injured by Aiyana. He died right there in a pool of blood.

Elvira now took advantage of this. She would make the colonel's death look like an accident and leave his body where it had impaled itself. She went to her room, packed her bags, and left the house. She planned to start a new life and left for London — but she did not forget that she still had to get her revenge against Salish and Aiyana.

Eleven years passed, and White Moon turned fourteen. She was mature and physically developed for her age. She had long black hair; striking dark eyes like black pearls, raised and arched eyebrows that penetrated those she did not know. She had rosy lips, an oval face with strong indigenous features, and an open and charming smile. She had the slender body of a young warrior girl. She wore a decorated tunic with an orange and brown design, with long fringes that fell from her long, slender arms. On her feet, she wore decorated moccasins made from buffalo hide.

Amitola was proud of his niece. Aiyana and Salish had trained White Moon in self-defense. She had mastered the bow and arrow and the tomahawk and could also mount and ride a horse very well without a saddle. She always accompanied Aiyana and taught the young indigenous girls to defend themselves against the white man and the animal predators in the forest. The Cherokee heiress spoke English perfectly, which she had learned from Salish, as well as Cherokee.

One autumn night, the stars were twinkling in an indigo blue sky and witnessed Utah's return. He was now twenty- three years old and now living with the white man. His habits had completely changed. Only his face and his hidden Cherokee identity remained. He was tall and strong, with black hair to his shoulders, and black eyes that expressed an honest and fearless gaze.

Utah had a secret in his heart. He was searching for White Moon's eyes in every Cherokee girl. After all those years, he wondered, how would he react on meeting the young princess Cherokee — the owner of his heart.

Amitola was surprised at his return and immediately celebrated with a big bonfire. Aiyana and Salish embraced their good friend and tribal brother. Utah was happy to be with them again and asked about White Moon, if she talked about him?

White Moon was serving corn, nuts, and fruit to the elders when she saw Utah again. She was thrilled and stunned when her eyes met his, and they were both filled with love and great happiness. It would appear that love had arrived for them both — very suddenly and quite unexpectedly. It took a while for Utah to believe that the beautiful young Native American was his Cherokee princess, who had been hidden in his own dream world. The young warrior and White Moon embraced and were both filled with great joy and happiness. Both their hearts throbbed together and they were full of a special love that came with the blessing of the Great Spirit. Aiyana and Salish were surprised about this fateful meeting. Aiyana now sensed that the time had come to have a conversation with White Moon.

The next day, Aiyana sat in her tribal position and with her nurturing and strong arms; hugged White Moon and said, "Today, you turn fourteen. I have done what I promised to the Great Spirit. I have taught you lessons about your indigenous roots. Try to be connected to the Great Spirit every day. From now on, you are fully responsible for all your actions. Today, I sensed that a new life is coming for you and things will change. If your destiny is to live with the white man again, go ahead. Don't be afraid of the unknown. I have prepared you as a warrior and the guardian of the Cherokee way of life."

"Grandma Aiyana, all this responsibility scares me, but I feel strong and I know I can face this new life that is coming. Why am I feeling the growing flames of love in my heart for Utah?"

"My Indian princess," the matriarch said. "Utah is as strong as a tree trunk, a warrior that can overcome most difficult situations on earth. The Great Spirit is wise and weaves our lives. He has already woven your passage on earth to work for the benefit of the indigenous, the white man, and every living creature you meet. Be guided and do what you feel is right."

Aiyana affectionately kissed the young girl's hands. White Moon reciprocated, lovingly kissing Aiyana's face. "Thank you, grandmother Aiyana, for your love and care over all these years. What would I be without you? And Salish, my adoptive mother, has sustained my heart. I remember the sad day I saw my father, White Wolf, killed by that white woman — a snake in the skin of a woman. Captain Harold, my white father, took me from the tribe to an unknown home. He beat Salish without pity or compassion. My heart was stripped by the death of my real father right in front of me. Grandmother Aiyana, I have two long thorns in my heart because of the death of my indigenous parents by the hands of the white man." Tears flowed copiously from the eyes of the young girl.

At that moment, Utah came toward them, and her sadness disappeared. Only the heart can explain what is unknown to reason. White Moon shyly grinned, her face brightening with the arrival of the prince of her heart.

The next day, White Moon went with Utah, sitting behind him on a horseback ride through the vast plains. She held him tightly as he galloped away. For both of them, time seemed to stand still. He felt her throbbing heart united with his, and they both cast out the cold air of the hills, which calmed their smitten and racing hearts. The lush green vegetation and the colorful wild flowers became more vibrant in the presence of these nature lovers. After riding for a while, Utah dismounted and led White Moon to the edge of a river.

White Moon walked to the river and noticed that Utah pulled out a bag made of buffalo leather and something that looked like a flute.

"I didn't know that you played the flute," she said, delightedly. "Oh yes," Utah answered. "I learned to play it from Dakota, a friend." With delicate movements, Utah played a sweet melodious tune to his beloved. She was enchanting at his mastery of this simple instrument. Its gentle sounds mingled with the light breeze over the rippling water, transporting them with the feeling of peace, harmony, and seduction. White Moon closed her eyes, trying to keep this magical moment to herself. When Utah stopped playing, he kissed her beautiful pink lips, both of them giving in completely. "Your lips are like pure honey," Utah said, happy to have discovered a pure indigenous love. "I now know why I could never forget you. You were so tiny and pure, being manipulated by Captain Harold, I knew your heart. Believe me, I saved myself for many years for this pure love. I just did not know that you would be the Indian princess of my heart."

They went swimming in the river and played like two innocent children all afternoon. After emerging, they lovingly touched each other when suddenly, White Moon cried out! She had noticed a curious red wolf on the other side of the river. Utah took White Moon's and gently led her back to his horse. They both got on, and she held him even tighter than before, and they headed back.

Amitola and Aiyana had convened a Tribal Council with the other key Cherokee chiefs for the following week.

Amitola was surprised that Utah had done all that he had said he would after he had left them. He had continued studying English and became an official translator for US Ethnic Affairs, communicating very well with the indigenous communities. He knew all the agreements that had been broken with the Native Americans, including those between White Wolf before his death and the other chiefs. Utah had come back because it was reported that the Cherokees were at risk of being massacred if gold was found in their territory.

Utah was surprised when he saw the tribe well-armed and with many horses. Being of mixed blood, Salish became a good businesswoman and brought hope, which appeared to have been lost. For all those years, she managed to sustain and support the tribe.

With a radiant sunset, arrived the chiefs. Amitola asked the rest of the tribe to stay in their village so as not to be bothered by anyone, because not all of them were prepared to hear the prophecy that night.

Amitola offered the sacred pipe to the leaders, who were already seated in their positions. After some time, Amitola started the meeting by kneeling on the ground with his eyes closed. He grabbed a handful of dirt and said, "The union with the Great Spirit is our strength to keep going." He began to prophesize.

"We will be betrayed, and the yellow metal will be found in our lands. We'll have to leave our territory for lands that are not productive. The white man will not follow any written agreements. After so much suffering and death, we will have to give up our land — our gift from the Great Spirit, to coexist peacefully with the white man, accepting the changes to survive on earth or be purged from this world forever. The blood of the indigenous nations will be taken by the Great Spirit."

Utah and one of the chiefs stood up at the same time to protest. "I don't accept everything I've heard," Utah said. "Maybe, I can try to change the story of the white man against us and make an alliance with the Europeans who embrace our cause. Due to everything I know, I may be able to provoke an Indian war! I will ask the Spanish and French for help. The English are united with the Americans."

Aiyana, surprised by the young Indian, was worried and rose to speak. "I don't know how to disobey the Great Spirit. Be careful. Your coexistence with the white man from other places on earth is influencing you and taking your indigenous roots. We cannot shed any more blood and change the destiny written by the Great Spirit. Mother Earth will cry for a while, giving painful birth with repeated contractions, causing tremors, upheaving soil, resulting in major disasters and deaths until the Great Spirit heals the incoming pain. This will be the price that the white man will have to pay."

Utah lowered his head, and the other indigenous leaders did not have the courage to challenge the tribal matriarch. Shaken, Amitola continued, "I believe we should negotiate our territory without the blood of the innocent drenching the earth. Leaving the territory that the Great Spirit gave us and being forced to go to unproductive land will be the biggest test of survival and humility that the Cherokees have ever faced. I want to be clothed by Mother Earth and enter the Great Spirit's land, where there is no pain and we do not suffer any bullets."

After everything was said, the indigenous chiefs were taken to the tents and comforted by the company of the tribal family. White Moon and others passed around handmade baskets filled with corn, baked potatoes, and fruit, and eventually, they all left to ponder the prophecy. Utah, even though he was sad, went to see White Moon.

The next day, after the chiefs left, everything remained quiet, until a large number of mounted army soldiers carrying an American flag arrived at the top of the mountains.

Captain Andrew was in command of the men, and he was accompanied by Elvira. Salish was near the road, teaching self-defense to small girls, when she saw the army coming. She cried out a warning to Amitola and Aiyana.

When Salish saw Elvira, she went into shock. Her legs buckled, and she fainted right there on the road.

Amitola saw everything. The Cherokee chief quickly called all the women to get their children and the warriors to take their positions. Warriors took their guns and ammunition — saved for this very moment — as well as their bows and arrows. This moment would be frozen in Earth's history.

The troop halted near Salish. Captain Andrew asked Elvira, "Who is this mixed-blood woman passed out on the ground? I don't accept people like this."

Surprised, one of the soldiers near the captain dismounted and said, "Captain, I saw her trading horses when I was buying thoroughbred horses for the army. The Spanish European traders didn't pay her any attention, but she caught my eye because of her green eyes, indigenous expression, and her attractive figure."

The captain was full of rage. "An American woman who also has Indian blood. Where did this madness come from? Now I understand how the Cherokee Indians have managed to defend themselves for so long. The mystery has now been revealed."

"Give me the right to settle the score with this mixed-blood enemy, who was my father's widow," Elvira said.

With a gun in hand, the captain accompanied Elvira.

Elvira approached Salish. Captain Andrew dismounted, taking a bottle of strong salts from his pocket, and removing its cap, he waved it under her nose.

She suddenly awoke, agitated, and with wide red eyes and a flushed face. Slowly, she got to her feet, and cold sweats took over her whole body.

"It seems like I got lucky. Revenge is as sweet as honey for those who know how to wait," said Elvira, angered.

Captain Andrew pointed the gun at Salish and said, "You mixed-blood mestiza Indian, you're arrested for negotiating and bringing weapons to the Cherokees. You will be judged and taken to the US Supreme Court."

The soldiers entered the camp and started shooting at the Indians. With showers of arrows and bullets they retaliated. But Utah and the warriors were outnumbered. There was no time to prepare other defenses. Many died. It was a massacre with bodies scattered everywhere.

White Moon, who was tucked away in one of the tents, took care of the women, old men, and children. Then a soldier came in with a rifle and pointed it at her. "Wow! What an Indian beauty. I'll kill everyone and be with you."

White Moon understood what he said and implied. "You do not know what you have got yourself into, white man," she protested. "I will rip your eyes out, pull your guts out, and give them to the antelopes to eat."

The soldier, taken aback by her retaliation in English — coming from an ignorant Indian! — let his gun point to the ground. With one strong kick, White Moon disarmed the soldier. But, he threw her brutally to the ground and kicked her. They fought. Then Aiyana threw a knife towards her. White Moon picked up the knife and stabbed the soldier in his abdomen, taking his life from him. Aiyana lifted White Moon, now battered and sore, and led everyone else to another safer tent.

Amitola beat many soldiers with his bow and knife. One of the soldiers with a rifle almost reached him.

Soldiers with rifles came through the tribe and entered where White Moon, the elders, children and women were hiding and began shooting without mercy or pity. A veil of smoke engulfed the air, which now smelt of gunpowder. There was total chaos.

Amitola, with a battered heart, felt that surrender was the only solution to prevent more deaths. He got the captain's attention and made a peace sign. Captain Andrew called for a ceasefire.

Now they had to negotiate once again with the US Government.

Aiyana went to look for Salish. She was surprised by Elvira's return. Elvira recognized Aiyana, watching the old matriarch getting close and holding the hand of White Moon, her father's adopted daughter. For a moment, she acknowledged that White Moon was an Indian princess and had stolen her place in her father's heart, and in a fit of jealousy and rage, she grabbed the gun and screamed.

"Salish, your time has come. I will send you and your Cherokee daughter to hell."

"You can dry my blood, but not my heart," Salish replied. "White Moon will not have that fate. Through the evil that you have done, today I have redeemed my identity as a white woman. I no longer hate you. I feel sorry for you! My native blood has helped me rescue the white woman who lives inside of me. I am at peace."

Elvira became even angrier at Salish's words and drew her gun to shoot White Moon. Salish unexpectedly threw herself at Elvira. Captain Andrew shot her and hit her right in the heart. Blood soaked her body. She died peacefully. An angelic expression, that of a duty fulfilled, pervaded her face. She had given her life for her daughter and she had died for what she had believed in.

Amitola was disturbed by the death of Salish. In defense of White Moon, he asked Utah to translate their surrender to the captain and negotiate the Cherokee territory.

"Cherokee chief," Captain Andrew spoke, "a few years ago, it was announced that there was gold in your territory, but there was no proof. This information just now got to the US Government. Your brother White Wolf drew a map on the ground, marking where the gold was before he died besides Captain Harold." From his coat pocket, he pulled out an old crumpled piece of paper with drawings on it. "If you want to live and for the good of your tribe, tell me where the gold is hidden. We have already decided that your tribe will be located to other places." Amitola bowed his head humbly and agreed to show where gold could be found.

Elvira did not relent when she saw White Moon crying desperately for Salish. "For many years," she said, "I have had this signed paper from the government for the Guardianship of Minors. This document authorizes me to send this Indian girl to a Christian College. She was taken from the Cherokee tribe and adopted by my father Harold, an American captain, and given the name Samira. She has just now lost Salish, her mixed-blood adoptive mother. I insist that the law be enforced and this minor be taken to a Christian boarding school that accepts Indian orphans."

The captain was appalled by Elvira's confession. He shook his head from side to side. It was hard for him to now believe that Captain Harold, who was so competent, could have been involved with a mixed-blood woman at his home! To make it even worse, he had an Indian as his daughter and named her Samira.

Aiyana did not understand what was happening, but was agonized on seeing White Moon with Elvira.

White Moon looked at the sky and asked for strength from the Great Spirit. And through the hundreds of native trees all around her, she felt Him sending her strength. She remembered the last conversation she had had with Aiyana. At that moment, the young, desperate, and battered Utah, for fear of losing his Indian princess, covered his face with his hands.

Captain Andrew pointed at White Moon and spoke, "Samira, you will go to a Christian boarding school for the time set by the law." He wrote on a piece of paper where she would be sent, signed it, and asked a sergeant to take the girl away.

Before the tribe was forcefully removed, Amitola had to show the captain were the gold was located.

Aiyana, with the courage of a warrior, remained emotionally strong. She understood that White Moon did not belong to her, but to the Great Spirit. She was aware that she had prepared her niece very well. Now, she would fulfill her destiny. She had to live with the white man again. After reflecting, Aiyana lifted her head and helped those in her tribe who were wounded in both body and soul.

Utah felt the sad bitter fate of being split from his beloved princess. He was injured, and deep in thought, he mounted his horse with a heavy heart and set off for the Indian reservation where he worked. There he would continue helping with the arrival of needy Native Americans. Yet nothing was going to stop him from finding his one true love once again.

White Moon's
Christian Discipline

White Moon sat at the back of the wagon, her personal items in the military bag, and although she was slightly injured and bruised, she did not complain. The trip was long, and she perked up when she saw a large eagle flying above her. It had a white head and white neck — it was the same one she had seen with her father in her dream. She sensed his spirit and knew she was not alone. The eagle accompanied them for quite a long time, much to the surprise and irritation of the sergeant.

"If this eagle continues to fly just above us, I will shoot it," shouted sergeant Tom.

White Moon, feeling that her father's protective eagle was in danger, whistled and said, "Wise eagle, fly far away from the white man. Tell my father, White Wolf, who lives in the sky, that I survived and am fine. The Great Spirit will give me strength to face this new life with the white man."

After hearing White Moon's words, the great eagle flew off far away, escaping the danger.

The narrow-minded sergeant, whose heart was as cold as stone, looked cruelly at the young Native American girl. "You Indians are crazier than I thought. You talk to wild animals. What did you say to it anyway? Because it flew right away and I didn't have the chance to shoot the thing."

"Only the Great Spirit can answer you," White Moon replied.

"You're lucky you speak English very well. A beating every day at this boarding school will teach you what is real and make you stop talking to animals," he said.

After the reprimand, White Moon was silent until she was told that they had arrived at the Christian boarding school. She got down from the wagon and was taken to talk to the school administrator. Mariana, the Principal, was a middle-aged woman, refined, somewhat haughty, and rather distant. White Moon thought that she behaved like a "colonel in a skirt!" Holding a paper in her hand, Mariana confirmed the accuracy of the document that Captain Andrew had signed.

Mariana was stunned by White Moon's arrival and by the fact that she also had the name Samira. She was completely taken aback when White Moon introduced herself.

"I speak English," she said. "Salish, my mother, was a mestiza, and I would like to continue wearing my indigenous clothes."

Mariana made notes in a book and, arranging her glasses on her face, said, "My name is Mariana and I am the Principal of this Christian boarding school, which is supported by the Christian Missions. Samira, the school will experiment with you because your father was an important US Army Captain and your mother was of mixed blood. It's worth investing in trying to transform you to fit into the American culture. I want to make it quite clear that I will give the orders and you will follow them. The rule here is that you listen and speak only when necessary. There must be complete obedience — no visits from outside except during vacations. You must be in class when the bell rings every day. You must be punctual always, including for Christian Religion classes. You will have classes in English, arithmetic, cleaning, cooking, and sewing. All types of indigenous pagan worship are prohibited in this institution. If you don't follow the schedule or fulfill your obligations, you will be punished and forced to work — to clean the entire school, for example. Do you understand? I think I have been very clear." She gestured with her right hand and sent Samira to a room with other girls of her age until a room could be found just for her.

Mariana turned and continued, "I will arrange for a doctor to come and treat your injuries. Now go and put on the uniform that you will be provided with. Indigenous clothing is not allowed here. You will wear this orphanage's uniform instead. If you have any questions, just ask for me."

White Moon was shaken by everything she had heard. She thought, *What are the obligations and rules Mariana was talking about?* She looked around and wondered where the other girls were. The place was as cold and sad as the white woman. There was nothing in the institution she could see that had anything to do with Mother Nature or the mountains. Everything was closed, and it made her feel like she was being suffocated.

Having been given her room and new uniform, she noticed a wooden frame above her bed — a picture of a man (Jesus) attached to it. It looked like the same picture that Salish had hung on her bedroom wall when she lived with Captain Harold, her white father. In her bedroom, there was dark, simple, and very clean wooden furniture in the old, refined, and tasteful English style.

White Moon was contemplating the picture of Jesus when she was interrupted by Judith, who, startled on seeing a Native American, cried, "Help! An Indian has escaped from her tribe and is hidden in my room." Grabbing a long-handled brush, Judith raised her right arm and prepared to attack White Moon just when Mariana came along with several excited young girls.

"What kind of aggression is this? she said. "Put that brush down, immediately! Turning to the other young girls, she said, "This is Samira, she is joining us from today. Please welcome her. She is the daughter of an American father and a mixed-race mother." White Moon realized that this place would be a serious challenge for her."

"I'm sorry," Judith said to Mariana. "I was just defending myself. I am the leader of the school, and I thought that this Indian was going to attack me."

White Moon gave Judith a harsh look and answered in perfect English, "Don't worry. I will prove to you that I am not a wild animal. Time will tell." Judith was very shocked to hear her speak such good English and shook her head from side to side. The other girls gathered around White Moon and introduced themselves.

Judith, it turned out, was Mariana's niece, and the daughter of an English father and an Irish mother. She was a tall girl, with blonde hair, light blue eyes, thin lips, and a rather sadistic expression. She was rather gangly and physically disconnected. Her father had killed her mother because he had caught her cheating on him.

He was arrested and convicted, but he hung himself in prison. When Mariana learned this tragedy, she brought her niece to the boarding school. As a single woman, she hoped her niece would be able to fill her empty heart.

The doctor came to White Moon's room. He introduced himself and began to take care of her wounds. He told Marina that the girl should be put on bedrest for a few days because she was suffering emotionally from the war and her recent losses.

A few days passed and White Moon remained melancholic. She spoke little and had difficulty eating the white man's food, which was very different from what she was used to, and it did not settle well with her. She was struggling to adapt. It was difficult for her to wear the uniform because it had a long skirt that covered her ankles and went till her feet. This restriction made it difficult for her to walk fast, and she also had to wear a long apron around her waist. The standard uniform was the same as that worn by the maidservants of the King of England. It was an emotional blow when she was forced to have her long black hair cut shorter. White Moon sensed that all of these changes were repressing her indigenous identity. When she walked, she lamented the lack of her hair, which she had never ever cut before.

It was a sunny spring afternoon, and the birds were preparing their nests in the trees. White Moon asked for permission to go to the courtyard and get some fresh air and see the many peach trees around the school.

To her astonishment, Judith appeared and tapped her on the shoulder. "It's time that you know who's in charge here. I am, you damned Indian! If you speak to Mariana, I will get you. I will make your life a living hell. In cooking classes, I don't clean. I always choose one of my friends to do it for me. When it's your turn, you will obey me and clean everything very well. Never say that I made you do it. If you tell, I will get you back the next day." Judith burst into laughter and left.

Mary, a poor orphan girl of fourteen, was listening to this behind a peach tree. She heard everything Judith had said and came towards White Moon. Mary was shaken by Judith's words. "I'm sorry," she said. "I shouldn't hide or eavesdrop. It is just that I really like you and want to help you. Life is not easy at this school. Judith hates Indians. She is dangerous and will get you if you don't do as she says."

Mary told White Moon that Mariana was Judith's aunt, and because of this, she turns a blind eye to whatever she does. She doesn't know that her niece is so horrible. "I want to tell you an important secret. Every Tuesday, Judith jumps over the school wall with the help of the other girls and climbs a wooden ladder and meets Alan. They are lovers. He is Father Edward's nephew and lives close to the school. White Moon, you speak English well. Here, we communicate through notes because we can't always talk. As you have seen, Mariana's staff is always watching us. I want to get to know you better; I have never believed everything they say about Indians. I think you are the true owners of the land. I can't say that out loud, or I would be punished and beaten by Judith."

White Moon smiled and replied sincerely. "Don't worry about Judith. For now, I can't show my strength."

"Do you know how to write?" Mary asked.

"I will learn how to write better," White Moon replied shyly. "I can write the basics because my mother Salish taught me. I hope you can help me improve. I stopped studying because my mission was to visit other villages and teach the young Native American girls to defend their chastity from the white man."

"What an honor it must have been to help other women," Mary said. She was a young woman of average height, slim, with emerald green eyes, a sweet expression, and light brown hair.

After this conversation, which rather shook White Moon, the bell rang and the girls were called for dinner. The smell of roasted and grilled meat filled the dining room.

The school's dining room was rather large and bare, and its large windows let in air and daylight as well as made the environment clean and warm. The tables were wide and long and covered with starched white tablecloths. Vases full of fragrant magnolias that filled the hall with a sweet, floral scent were on each table. Edwina, the kind cook, had a cheerful disposition. She was jolly by nature and always seemed to be happy.

Every afternoon, Edwina made a delicious snack with tea and homemade bread for the girls. After dinner, she finished her work and left the cleaning to the girls. After White Moon's arrival, the other girls hardly ever cleaned the kitchen anymore.

White Moon began her tasks at six o'clock in the morning. After her classes were finished, she scrubbed the floor almost every day — on her hands and knees and with a big scrubbing brush. Soon, her knees became sore, reflecting the pain and injustice she was experiencing in this situation imposed on her by the white man.

White Moon was always attentive to the schedule. When it was time to switch classes, she forgot the freedom she had in the mountains of Georgia. She hated the brass bell and the control that Mariana had over her. When she went to sleep, she prayed to the Great Spirit to hear from Utah, Aiyana, and Amitola.

After her afternoon snack, White Moon was called to confess to Father Edward. The indigenous princess refused to give up her roots and become someone she was not.

She went to the confessional not knowing what was going to happen. The priest, with his eyes fixed on the young girl holding a bible in her right hand, said, "Samira, I see you're doing well. Unlike in controlled Indian reservations that I have seen, you do not mind complying with the rules. Why do you still resist going to Mass and confession?"

"Father," she replied. "I have nothing against it, but I'm not ready to be forced to do something that I still don't understand."

"I want to make it clear to you that if you keep resisting to change your religion, unfortunately, I will be obliged to notify Mariana and your punishment will be doubled. There will be severe consequences."

She broke into a cold sweat when the priest mentioned more punishment. She looked up and defended herself. "I feel strong like a tree. I stay strong even when pain and loneliness take over my heart. I want to meet that man impaled on the cross. He has a sweet look on his face and he, in some way, moves me. I sense that he is connected to our Great Spirit. Father Edward, I still don't understand why the white man is better than us because they put that man on a frame and killed him."

The priest opened his eyes wide and raised an eyebrow, surprised by such a wise response from the young girl. "My daughter, it seems that you are finding the answers from your Great Spirit through the presence of Jesus deep in your heart." Thrilled and surprised, his eyes brimming with tears, the priest shook his head from side to side. He opened several passages of the Bible and began to talk about Jesus — the man who was nailed to the cross by the white men. White Moon loved the Bible passages read by the Priest. Soon, the school bell rang.

Outside the front entrance, the priest's nephew got down from the school's buggy and walked towards the patio. Surprised, he bumped into White Moon coming out of the door. The priest was just behind her.

Alan spoke lasciviously to the priest after she passed. "Wow! What pure beauty! This is the Indian that Mariana has been hiding at the school. Judith is nothing like as attractive as this Indian. Her bountiful Indian breasts must be warm and nurturing. Indians are like street dogs, what is she doing here? Mariana and the missions should not invest money on ignorant Indians. The US Government should spend more money on weapons to exterminate them all. If I were not your nephew, I would have her take Judith's place for a while."

At this outburst from his nephew, the priest grew furious and shouted, "Get out of here, you idiot! You have done enough damage with Judith already. I've told you not to come here. You're disgusting and perverted. Your vulgarity and lack of decency with women will be your undoing and imprisonment. Learn to respect the Indians! You will burn in hell!"

Alan got away from his uncle as fast as he could, punching the air, unmoved by his reprimand.

Night came and Judith went to meet her lover as usual. And White Moon stayed up late, cleaning the kitchen and polishing the pots.

To take revenge on his uncle and make Judith jealous, Alan told her that he met White Moon in the schoolyard and that she was the most beautiful and seductive Indian girl he had ever seen and that no white woman could even compare to her. After meeting Alan, Judith was furious and vowed to "tear off White Moon's skin with her own hands".

A few turbulent days went by at the school. White Moon was scheduled to make lunch with Edwina's help. Judith kept her eyes on the kitchen the whole time. At a certain point, the cook asked White Moon to go to the pantry and get some supplies. Taking the opportunity, Judith poured a packet of salt into the large soup pan that White Moon was preparing on the stove.

Soon all the girls and the staff came into the dining room and sat down to have lunch. Judith, with an air of maliciousness said, "Let's give Samira a hand! Today, for the first time, she has cooked us a wonderful pea soup. With this cold outside, there is nothing better than a bowl of hot soup. Mariana, please try Samira's soup."

Mariana was enthusiastic at her niece's praise and put a spoonful of the soup in her mouth. She instantly spat it out and knocked the bowl over on the table much to everybody's amusement! Humiliated in front of everybody, with so much salt in her mouth, she could barely even scream. "White Moon," she said, determined to punish her severely.

"You have been here long enough, and you can't even make a simple soup for us all to eat? Go to your room right now and think about what you have done. For fifteen days, you will not go to your regular classes. Instead, you will clean the entire school. I can now give the cleaners a break, and you will not have your afternoon snack or the apple pies that you so enjoy. You will also work in the laundry. You must starch and iron all the students' uniforms. What a terrible investment for me and the missionaries in trying to make you a white woman." White Moon, humiliated, listened and left with her head down. She thought about what happened and knew that it must have been Judith's doing. Father Edward learned about the episode from Mary, White Moon's close friend, who confessed about Judith's evildoings. The priest asked Mary to take boiled corn, apple tarts, and hot milk to White Moon without Mariana finding out and said that he would help in whatever way possible.

White Moon was feeling very depressed, but some good news finally came.

Mariana was surprised by the arrival of Captain Andrew, her childhood friend, with a military convoy. To her complete amazement, the captain was escorting a young Native American.

The captain quickly hugged his old friend and said, "Are we too late for your wonderful English afternoon tea? I've heard that you have a cook who makes excellent apple pie — like those made for the King of England. I want to introduce you to an Indian friend who has helped me on the reservations. He has studied the law and helps the American Federal Agents that care for Indigenous Affairs." Utah, with a confident look on his face, shook Mariana's hand. Captain Andrew left them alone and went to enjoy the wonderful scent of the magnolias in the garden.

Utah, quite sure of himself, said, "Madam Mariana, I have worked with Captain Andrew for a year now on the guardianship document that sent White Moon as Samira to this institution. As an Agent of Indian Affairs in this country, I ask permission to visit White Moon on holidays until she comes of age. I ask that you do not oppose this request because I have acquired this right from the Governor and the English and French Christian Missions."

Mariana was amazed by the Indian's attitude, his command of the English language, and his obvious confidence. She had never come across such a polished and well-educated Indian with so much knowledge of American law. How did he get into this legal position? The Principal did not know what to do in this situation, especially now that she had just given the girl such a severe punishment. How would she explain herself if the missions found out? She would be reprimanded or fired from her position.

Mariana unhesitatingly called for Samira and guided Utah to a small and quiet room where she left him to wait for her.

White Moon arrived and knocked at the door. To her surprise and amazement, Utah opened the door. The lovers' eyes met and White Moon's heart skipped a beat and immediately throbbed with happiness. Her soul mate had truly fulfilled his promise. Utah gave her a very tight hug.

He was very surprised to see White Moon with her hair cut short. "What happened to your hair, my Indian princess?"

"As soon as I arrived here, they cut it," she said shyly. "It was very difficult for me to renounce my indigenous identity. But I've now got used to walking with this long dress and apron that the white women use. How did you find me at this school?"

"I've been looking for you the whole time. Then, one day, when I was feeling heartbroken, I was assigned to work on this particular Indian reservation. With the help of the Great Spirit, Captain Andrew recognized me from when he captured our Cherokee tribe. To my surprise, he asked me for help with issues between the Federal Government and the native chiefs. He promised me that if I finished my work with the indigenous leaders, he would personally bring me here. We both did our part."

White Moon, quite overwhelmed and with all the emotion of the moment, started crying. "What happened to Aiyana, Amitola, and our Cherokee tribe?"

"My beloved princess, I have to tell you that unfortunately Amitola was pressured by the military and forced to take the Cherokees away from Georgia. They signed a treaty and were sent to Oklahoma. I followed the process from afar to ensure their rights to land ownership from the British and the French. The worst part was the devastating journey, the so-called "Trail of Tears". The sorrow and pain that everyone had to go through because they saw all of their dreams destroyed. Your father White Wolf's premonitions were right. Our Cherokee tribe became bitter with their misfortune. They suffered hunger, death from smallpox and other disease like influenza, and the destruction of their very souls and being. Unfortunately, I have to tell you that Aiyana died in her sleep after having completed her mission to bring our people across the "Trail of Tears" to Oklahoma."

White Moon was shocked to hear about Aiyana's death and the suffering of the Cherokees. It was hard for Utah to see her in pain. She was very upset, tearful, and sobbing. He spoke optimistically, "My beloved Indian princess, all is not lost because you're alive and studying. Even though it's against the tribal will, the Great Spirit knows what he is doing and will continue to guide the Cherokees."

"Yes, it's true, Utah," White Moon responded and sighed. They exchanged caresses for a long time until Mariana arrived. They separated and their mood changed.

"Sir, Utah, your time is over, will you please take your leave? Unfortunately, this institution is for orphaned girls, and you cannot stay here overnight. You can schedule a time during Samira's vacation to return."

Utah, like a true gentleman and honest politician, responded. "Madam Mariana, I want to be informed of everything that happens with Samira. I noticed injuries on her arms due to forced labor and her knees are severely bruised. What is happening in this institution? I'll be back for her vacation and if my ward is not being properly cared for and respected like a Native American here, I will be forced to denounce this Christian Institution to the highest-ranking Missionaries in this country. We may have lost the war, but you have not eliminated our Native American honor or dignity. Do we have a deal, ma'am?" Mariana did not respond.

Utah left. Mariana felt attacked; her pride was wounded. "Did you report me?" She demanded from White Moon. "The freedom you so desperately need, will cost you dearly. You will only get out of here the way I want. I wish I could kill the strong Indian identity that lives within you."

"Only now have I really met you," White Moon replied. "I did not tell Utah all the bad things and injustices I have suffered here. He saw my injuries with his own eyes. I did not have to say anything. Who knows, but maybe you will need my Indian identity at this school. I will not fight back against this hatred you have towards me. I only believe in the good!"

Mariana accepted this, accepted that Samira was different from all the other orphan girls who had gone through the school. Samira spoke from her heart.

White Moon tearfully walked to the flower gardens and contemplated the arrival of spring with new shoots of daisies and yellow roses. To her surprise, she saw two men from the Italian Mission erecting a sculpture of the Virgin Mary. The Madonna wore a light blue cloak and her eyes conveyed peace and love. Her head held a beautiful crown of flowers picked from the school garden.

The Blessed Virgin held a contented baby Jesus in her arms. Her feet were covered with white and yellow fragrant roses that gave off a strong smell throughout the courtyard. White Moon was very sensitive and thought, *Through this iconic image, peace has returned to my heart.*

The school bell rang and Judith came over to meet with White Moon. "I am almost ready to kill you, Samira," Judith shouted. "I forbid you to get close to Alan. As if, all of the cleaning you are forced to do was not enough. Don't try to see what else I am capable of. Keep to yourself. You are a chicken."

"Don't provoke me, you white rattlesnake," White Moon responded calmly. "I'm a volcano that is still under control. I will settle the score with you only when the time comes. I am not the one who jumps the fence and sneaks out after dark. You are the chicken, not me." White Moon, more calm and unruffled, left her antagonist talking to herself alone and went to the laundry room to finish ironing the uniforms.

After she finished her work, Edwina called White Moon. She was pleasantly surprised when she learned that Mariana, after Utah's critique, now allowed White Moon to have afternoon tea.

When she entered the dining room, White Moon felt the fresh air — filled with the smell of magnolias that came from the garden outside and mingled with aromas of citrus fruit peels, teas, and sweets — caress her face. Edwina took some warm bread from the oven — it was going to be even more delicious when served with her strawberry jam.

Edwina served her a bountiful afternoon snack. Wiping her hands on her long white apron, preoccupied, and with a heavy heart, she said, "Samira, my dear, I need to tell someone, and you are the only person with a clear enough head to listen. Through one of the windows in the kitchen pantry, I can see who goes by the front of the school. Recently, I saw two scruffy men prowling around the building. I believe that they were up to no good and are maybe looking to steal. After Mariana pays all of the bills for this school, she is responsible for distributing money to the other Christian schools. I think that these men are definitely thieves and have perhaps their eye on the school's money."

White Moon, worried about what she heard, shook her head. "Edwina, I don't think that the school is well protected from such people."

"Mariana is very secretive. She does not speak of administrative matters with anyone but relies on Captain Andrew, her best friend, and Mr. Mark Rossetti, the head of the Christian Missions. The only thing I know is that she keeps military weapons in the basement of the school, but I don't know if she knows how to handle these firearms."

"Edwina, don't worry. I'll go to the basement to see what kind of weapons there are to protect the school. If there are weapons, then we can protect ourselves."

The cook did not understand the young girl. "Why are you so interested in seeing the weapons?"

White Moon smiled and answered, "For now, I can't tell you."

The cook was relieved and gave White Moon a little hug. She smiled and said, "Don't tell anyone about what I have told you. I must get back to my work because Father Edward will have Mass at six o'clock in the chapel."

White Moon left quickly towards her well-deserved freedom, recalling the last moments she had spent with her beloved Utah.

The next day dawned and Judith awoke agitated, punching the air as if she were doing so to White Moon. She was inconsolable when she learned that Alan had a crush on the Native American. He, apparently, never got tired of praising White Moon's indigenous beauty.

The day passed quietly and uneventfully. After dinner, Judith was told by one of the girls that Alan needed to speak to her urgently. In the middle of the night, fearing that Mariana would see her, she jumped the school's high wall with the help of one of the other girls, her another victim.

She knocked on his door and when he opened it, she was startled. Alan had a knife in his hand. Judith, for the first time in her life, felt a shiver run through her entire body. Her voice screeched and she said, "Is this how you welcome me?" Alan acted like he didn't understand. "I didn't call you here for passion. I am asking you to prove your love for me." Alan put the knife to her throat and continued, "If you still want to be with me, you must do what I say before I kill you. I can find someone younger than you in the school to warm my bed in the winter."

Judith, now frightened, broke into a cold sweat and cringed.

"What do I have to do?" she said, her body pressed against the wall.

Alan, maliciously and cruelly, ran the knife along the girl's chest. "I need to know the day and time of the train that arrives with the delivery from the European Missions later this month."

"I don't know anything about that," Judith protested.

"You are getting on my nerves with your attitude. Don't play stupid, you slut. Your aunt is the principal of the school. Do you think I don't know that every month the Missions deliver provisions and money to her to distribute and deliver to the other schools?"

Judith became very nervous. "If my aunt never talks about her work with anyone, who told you about what happens at the school?"

"I have my sources. Do we have a deal? Now go. When you find out the information, I need you to come and tell me. I don't want to see you before that, do you understand?" Alan lowered his knife and opened the door for her to leave.

With her head lowered, it took Judith a while to really believe that Alan was using her to get information about the school. She thought, *Alan, with that knife in his hand, wasn't the lover she thought he was. Oh, how that wolf in sheep's clothing had fooled her.* Judith ran for the wall and fell, scraping both her knees.

The day had already dawned; it was almost six o'clock in the morning. Nobody was there to help her with the ladder, which was hidden behind a peach tree. Judith moaned and pulled herself up with a great deal of pain. When she got near the schoolyard, she bumped into White Moon, who had been unable to sleep and had gone for a walk around the yard to take in the fresh morning air.

White Moon felt the negative energy go right through her body when she saw Judith, who was bruised and bleeding. She was not surprised, for she knew that Judith had spent the night with that bad fellow. Nonetheless, she was discreet.

"Do you need any help?" she asked.

"Go to hell, you damned Indian! Go back to your tribe, your rightful place; my friends don't want you here. Mary is the only one who is not afraid of getting beaten up by me and likes you. Most Americans hate Indians. I am part of this group." Even injured and bleeding, Judith continued cursing White Moon with her sharp tongue.

That day, White Moon decided that she was tired of being hurt and the target of physical and emotional abuse and unable to react — this was not sustainable. Even if she tried to be like a white woman, just like the other girls from school, it was still difficult to live at the school and with Mariana. The girls did not stop attacking her Native American identity. For a moment, she examined her life and thought: *The white man is the foreigner in this land. When they arrived in the Cherokee territory, we were already living there. It is our inheritance from the Great Spirit and Mother Earth that sheltered us. The army took our land by force, yet Mother Earth teaches us not to retaliate with hate. So, the Cherokee Indians should be valued for our culture and conservation, and respect for the land.* With these thoughts, she returned to her room, and feeling tired, she lay down and had a pleasant sleep.

Father Edward found out from one of the girls through confession about the dangerous and scandalous encounters between his nephew and Judith. He knew of the risk and the danger the girl was in, but he was unable to do anything because he was a priest. The seal of confession had to be respected, but he had to do something to save the other girls from his nephew's clutches.

That same morning, Father Edward was called for by Mariana. He recognized the scent of sweet English lavender that filled the hallway, indicating her strict and domineering manner. Mariana, with a very serious look on her face, asked him a question.

"Father, I need to know the whole truth regarding Judith. Who is my niece involved with? Coincidentally, today I crossed the yard and came across a long ladder on the back wall of the school. Someone had tried to jump the wall and got hurt.

There were still small bloodstains on the ground. Today I went to Judith's room and was amazed to see that her knees were cut and bruised. Father, for God's sake, what's happening? Have I lost control of this school or the ability to control my niece? What was I thinking of by bringing Judith to this place? I, who have always exhibited only exemplary and dignified conduct in the Christian Missions, now have to turn a blind eye to protect her." Mariana was hurt and covered her face with her hands and wept a tear of shame.

Father Edward warmly took her hands and comforted her. "Unfortunately, we both have very similar problems. I wish you would not permit my nephew Alan into this institution. He lives alone on the outskirts of the school. It is not good for him to wander around here. I know Alan is a great carpenter and you call him when you need him, but I have sometimes caught him making eyes and having improper conversations with Judith and other girls. You don't know how difficult it is for me to live with my nephew's misconduct. The bad words he always uses hurt my ears and make me sick. My sister died when he was sixteen, and I took him in to live with me. He stayed with me for three years and learned the craft of carpentry in the institution where I was the priest and took care of the boys.

Unfortunately, my nephew fled, and after a few years, and due to the irony of destiny, when I was arriving at this school in the buggy, I came across him, asking you for work as a carpenter. Despite being young, he excels at his work. It takes a while for Alan to reveal that he is a cunning fox with evil intentions. What can I expect from a person who has exiled Christ from his heart?"

After hearing this, Mariana felt hot and flushed. She wiped her face and forehead with the back of her hand and said, "What horrible timing, now that I have delegated all of the carpentry work to Alan. I'll take serious measures and keep Alan out of the school. Father, to change the subject, I want you to accompany the arrival of the delivery from Europe next Monday. I'm going to need your help. This time, I cannot call the people from outside the school. Confidentiality shall be maintained and kept by us both."

The priest was happy with the confidence placed in him by Mariana and nodding his agreement. "It is an honor to work for the Christian Missions and be able to help others. You can count on my help."

Mariana gave him a piece of paper with all the schedules on it — a big mistake!

After the afternoon snack, Edwina gave White Moon the key to the basement. She put it in her apron pocket so that no one could see it. Worried, she kept an eye on the back entrance to avoid being seen by Mariana. She had to find out about the school's security with her own eyes.

Eagle-eyed, she walked down towards the narrow basement. She removed the key from her apron and opened the basement door. White Moon realized that, on the right side of the basement stairs, there was a small secret door. She went down the stairs with ease and opened it. Once she entered the secret basement, she was surprised at seeing a mahogany cabinet holding several guns as well as shelves filled with food. At the end of the basement, there was a built-in closet that was locked. White Moon took a good look at the weapons. She noticed they were similar to the weapons

Salish had purchased from the European dealers. Tears welled up in her eyes at the memory and longing she felt for her adoptive mother, grandmother Aiyana, and the Cherokee Mountains.

With her eyes glued on the hallway above her, she heard footsteps coming. She could see the shadow of a man with a hat trying to force the lock.

For a moment, White Moon, even though she was really worried and distraught, turned her attention from the door when she felt a big rat around her feet. She quickly grabbed its tail and hit it with her hand. The apparent thief had used a chair to climb up to the window and had forced the latch and opened it. Unseen, White Moon quickly hurled the rat at the thief's feet and made the sound of a wild bear to scare him even more. The man quickly dropped the bolt from the window and screamed.

"Where the hell did that come from? A bear inside as well! To hell with the missions' money." The terrified thief fled down the dark corridor and jumped over the high wall of the school, cursing as he went. White Moon laughed to herself in the basement. She admitted to herself that she had a wild impulsiveness that the white man did not understand.

She knew that Edwina was right. There were other people who knew about this place. It was a target for thieves. She concluded that the school was completely vulnerable to theft. She was worried and went outside for some fresh air around the peach trees. Mary, who was sitting on the grass starring at the sunset, hurriedly ran up to meet her friend.

Mary got straight to the point.

"My dear friend! I've been looking for you all over the school. Where have you been? I have news. Judith is hurt. I went to visit her, and she asked me how I learned to defend myself. Before she got hurt, she tried to hit me because I had refused to hide the ladder for her when she went to meet with Alan. I hit her right back! After so many beatings and humiliations, for the first time I felt worthy." Mary cried tears of joy and then wiped them with her starched white apron.

"Yes, I know how important dignity is for us in our lives, my friend!" White Moon said. "Unfortunately, the battle with Judith is not yet over at this school. I am counting on your help because I sense that something very bad is going to happen in the school's basement. I'm going to need your help early tomorrow, before the rooster crows. We'll go to the basement. I will teach you how to handle a gun."

Worried and surprised, Mary asked, "You'll what? I don't understand."

"Yes, you heard me right. Father Edward is waiting for us for confession. Please be discreet and don't tell our secret to anyone! Do you understand?"

"Yes, you better know what you're doing."

"I always know what I am doing when I have to protect my tribe, and you are part of it even though you are white. I had a vision that the Great Spirit will use me for an important test in this Christian institution."

Mary, without really understanding what White Moon told her, left quickly to fulfill her obligations. Father Edward was preparing for the evening Mass. He removed his cassock and put on lighter clothing. Without knocking, Judith barged into his room. Surprised by Judith's behavior, Father Edward swiveled around on his chair. He was carless and let the key to the basement and the paper with the schedule of the delivery drop from his lap. Irritated, he scolded her.

"Where are your manners? Don't you have any respect for the rules of conduct in this institution? Just because you're Mariana's niece doesn't mean you can do whatever you want. Now go out and knock on the door properly."

Judith justified herself. "I'm sorry!" She put her head down and pretended to be humble. Unfortunately, she noticed the paper and the key under the priest's chair. She looked at it, reading it out of the corner of her eye so as not to draw his attention, and understood what it was for. Cunning as a fox, she continued talking. "Father, my head is exploding with pain. Please, I ask that you let me do my confession another day. Right now, I urgently need to see a doctor." Pretending to faint, she fell to the ground.

The priest ran out of his room to find the school's doctor. Judith quickly opened her eyes and picked up the key and the paper and hid them in her apron pocket. When Mariana arrived with Doctor Joseph and the priest a couple of minutes later, she threw herself on the ground again. The doctor examined her and confirmed that the girl was fine and 'putting on an act'. From his bag, he soaked a cotton ball with a red pepper mixture from a bottle in his bag and rubbed it under the girl's nose. It forced her to open her eyes, which immediately became red.

"Damn chilli pepper," Judith cried. "Go to hell and rub this hot pepper in the eyes of the devil." She got up, cursing him.

The doctor went after her and grabbed her by the arm and brought her back.

"You still don't know my diagnosis," he said. "I use this to cure malingerers and fraudsters like you. I have to waste my time punishing manipulative brats like you who beat innocent girls so as to go and have secret meetings with their lovers. Now, the mystery of the girls with bruises on their bodies has been revealed. They were beaten and they told me it was an accident because they were scared of you. In time, I found out the truth. When you fell down by the wall and I was called to help, I was suspicious. But I never thought it would come to this point. Mary told me the whole truth."

Judith's eyes were swollen and burning. She broke her arm free from the doctor's strong grip. "If you were my daughter, I would give you a good beating and punish you for a long time. I would lock you in a room, and you wouldn't see the light of day."

The mask of lies of being a nice girl fell. Judith, now fearing a beating from the principal after the doctor's scolding, ran to her room. Mariana was very embarrassed by her niece's conduct and apologized to the doctor and shed a tear because it appeared that everyone except the principal of the school knew about her behavior. The doctor returned to the school's infirmary.

To calm Mariana, the priest changed the subject and asked her to go to Mass before dinner.

Young White Moon, worried about all that happened, and what was going to happen, went to her room early. The window was open and she watched the arrival of the full moon, illuminating everything in a bright light. The stars circled around in the dark indigo sky, awakening a magical time. With the fresh air that came through the window, she quickly fell into a deep sleep.

Soon, the figure of a mysterious white woman in her room sent a warm sensation through her body. The woman had hair of gold. White Moon was surprised and observed that her hair had curls that were held in place by gemstones, sapphires, and diamonds. She had a sweet and a fine complexion, and lively and penetrating deep blue eyes.

The young girl cringed when the delicate woman spoke. "Don't be afraid. I am the White Mother of the United Kingdom. I am also the Mother of all Native American Indians and all of those who live on the earth. I get my power from God the Creator, who feeds and nourishes all. White Moon, your mission is to make the white man, through your conduct, see me and learn to take care of me. I give everyone everything through the Creator, without asking for anything in return. Teach everyone I'm the same Mother who embraces all the children of the earth, without distinction of race or color." White Moon felt supported and protected by the energy that emanated from the White Mother. She continued, "Daughter of the Earth, union strengthens me while division between my children wounds me deeply. It dries my Divine milk, while my painful tears shake the bowels of the earth. I feed my children with the fruits of my own nature. I am the Mother that shelters all, but few take care of me. I can't continue to give shelter and live if my children go against me and destroy me. If that happens, I'll be cold, dry, and have no more milk to feed my young. I am present in all nations and races. I get energy from the Creator, and in my placenta, I receive life. At the transition to death, I gather the remains, clean them, and always transcend the energy. There is always renewal and transmutation."

The young girl listened to everything quite perplexed. The presence of the White Mother and everything she said was a revelation. For a moment, she simply stared at her and though to herself, *Am I going crazy?*

The White Mother read her mind, smiled, and said, "What you see is real. I'll leave a gift to remember me by." From the White Mother's hand, there appeared a large diamond that she gave to White Moon. Outside the window, she could see an angel with indigo blue eyes smiling at her. White Moon acknowledged that it was the same angel whom she had dreamed of having held her hands and those of all of the other children when she was a child.

It was not long after that someone began tapping on the door and White Moon awoke from her deep sleep.

"It's Mary. Can I come in? I need to talk to you urgently." "Yes," White Moon replied. "Please come in."

Seeing the diamond in her hand, the young girl shuddered in amazement. White Moon was deep in thought. *Aiyana, when they were in the Cherokee territory, had revealed a secret. When she was born, the tribe was taken and brutally massacred by the white man and the diamond that White Wolf was going to give her was stolen. Did Aiyana tell me the whole story?*

Mary, seeing her friend deep in thought, asked White Moon what was going on. "It seems that you are still dreaming; am I talking to myself?" Dazzled by the diamond in her friend's hand, she asked,

"Wherever did you get that huge diamond? Hide it before someone steals it from you." Mary did not give her friend a chance to explain what had happened and went right to the point. "I came here to warn you that the priest is desperate because he has lost the basement key and a paper with important information that the principal gave him. Last night, he asked me to look through the whole school for it."

"Yes, you can count on me!" White Moon said. "And don't forget that at six in the morning, down in the basement, I will teach you how to handle a gun. Now go back to bed, it is still too early."

Mary left the room. White Moon was worried about the news. "The priest who is always so dutiful with everything had not been so careful this time." She sensed that a battle was about to begin. She took the diamond and hid it. After all, it appeared that this place was not safe.

Near the front door, Judith, walking on her tiptoes, almost ran into Mary, and she quickly hid and got out of her way. Judith opened the front door, her head covered by a scarf, and ran to her lover's house.

Alan had not been able to sleep because the full moon had bothered him. He was about to close the window when he saw Judith arriving. He was surprised and went outside to make fun of her. "At last you appear. I thought your cowardice was greater than your love for me. Or have you come to feel the delights of passion?" Alan was soon tearing off Judith's night clothes and caressing her body. Judith pushed him away and threw the paper and the key at him.

"I have paid a very high price to have you. If you betray my trust, you will meet the most venomous snake on this earth. Here is when the next train will arrive with the shipment delivery from Europe. It seems that it will be packed with goods and lots of money to be distributed by my aunt. That is all I know for now."

The boy's eyes sparkled. He rubbed his hands together with glee, and grabbing the paper and key, he burst into laughter. With his eyes glued to the paper, he said, "Now it is my turn to leave this misery I live in. I have it all planned out with my army friends. They are well-armed. Next Monday, whoever lives will be a witness, because this Boarding School will go up in smoke."

"For God's sake," Judith cried. "Have you lost your mind?" "Don't get God involved in this," Alan said. "He should be well occupied with the affairs of the Church. Living in poverty is a cold and hard war for survival. I deserve to have a position of luxury and power. I am not fool enough to waste my time and follow my uncle's teachings. Keep quiet and I give you my word — get all your stuff and I will take you with me. With all the money from the robbery and goods, we will go to Ireland. There, I'll marry you, and nobody will know how I got the money."

Happy with what she heard, Judith threw herself into Alan's arms and let herself be taken by passion and lust. As the day was dawning, Judith returned to school unseen and feeling victorious because Alan had proposed.

White Moon and Mary met in the basement. Mary was yawning. "I see that you are not interested in what I am about to teach you. Pay more attention! Guns kill. There is no going back if you don't have firm hands and a steady eye. Please, wake up! I'm going to need you if something goes wrong. I will not be able to do this job alone, our lives and all the girls' lives are in our hands."

Mary, though she had been reprimanded by her friend, responded, "I cannot be as tough as you. God, help me!"

"The Great Spirit will only help you when you place all of your attention on what you are doing. I'll find out when the train will come in from Europe. This way, you'll have more time to practice." The two friends left the basement and were careful not to be seen.

White Moon was walking around the peach trees when Father Edward called for them. He had stumbled on a large, dead branch and asked for help to move it. "What are you girls doing here? Have you by any chance found my key?

Although, there really is no need to worry. Edwina had a spare that she already gave me. I told Mariana and she did not care. Concerning the paper, I have managed to memorize everything about the delivery on Monday afternoon."

Mary winked at White Moon who nodded in response. There was enough time for her not to disappoint her friend. The priest looked sadly at White Moon. "Unfortunately, I don't have good news for you about the Christian Missions. The American Court recently announced that the Cherokee land belongs to them, and the American military forces forced them off. Last winter, thousands died on their way to their new territory. With this total and complete humiliation of their indigenous identity, they suffered terribly with the cold, hunger, and pain. When they finally got to Oklahoma, the soil was not fertile enough to plant seed for their survival."

The indignant priest raised his hands to the sky and cried, "God, it seems like the persecution of Christ on earth again. I made a decision of my own; I have asked permission to be a part of these Missions. When you turn eighteen, which will be next month, I'll take you to your Indian reservation personally. I can see that God needs me more there than here in this institution. White Moon, through you I have learned that the Great Spirit of the Cherokee Indians is the same as the God of Heaven and Earth. I think I can learn much from the Cherokees, especially to stop all this suffering and continue honoring the Great Spirit. I hope to take the teachings of Jesus Christ to everyone."

White Moon was surprised with the priest's unexpected confession as well the emotions he displayed.

"Father, your words are like ripe fruits for me to enjoy. Only now, through your teachings, can I feel the truth of Christ in my heart." She knelt under a native fruit tree and prayed.

"Thank you, Great Spirit. Through the evil of the white man, we, the Cherokee Indians, have a place with Christ in Heaven, where the fruits of His teachings are savored by all who carry the cross on earth."

The school bell rang, and the three of them, happy with the love they shared, left to fulfill their obligations for the day.

Emancipation of White Moon and Return to Her Indigenous Roots

The next few days passed peacefully and new girls arrived in the school. Mariana always had her eye on Judith. After the incident with the doctor, for two days she was grounded in her room, where she stayed by herself, was constantly checked upon, and made to think about the consequences of her actions.

White Moon took some guns from the basement, wrapped them in cleaning rags, and camouflaged them behind some trees. The other guns she hid near the basement, where the rats lived and nobody dared to go.

Monday morning was clear, but dense and heavy clouds rolled in after lunch. White Moon faked illness to be excused from her sewing class. Mariana was worried about the girl and asked her, "For some time now, it seems that you are sad, worried, and isolated from everyone."

"Unfortunately, I have not received good news from my tribe," White Moon answered quietly. "I believe that the wounds will heal in time."

Mariana agreed and hugged her. "My dear, there is nothing better than time to heal the pain of loss. How can I help you?"

White Moon pulled out a small paper from her apron pocket and wrote a note addressed to Utah in Cherokee. At Mariana's sudden compassion, she was surprised but grateful and smiled. "Thank you! Please send this message as soon as possible by telegraph. I really miss Utah."

"I hope I can write these words in Cherokee on my telegraph." The principal left happy, having confirmed that there was something going on between the two of them.

White Moon excused herself and walked to her room. She brought out her native clothes that she had worn when she had arrived at the school and put them in a bag and hid them in the basement. When she got there, she immediately took off her dress and apron and put on the colorful tunic and moccasins. She painted her face with natural brown dyes to warn the thieves and indicate that she was hostile towards them. With a rifle in hand, she came out from the basement and went to the nearby peach trees.

The dense clouds continued to roll in, announcing a heavy storm. At three o'clock, the school bell rang, and all the girls lined up to go out to the schoolyard. Mariana, a notebook in hand, took attendance and realized that White Moon was not there. But everyone's attention was diverted by the arrival of the mission's wagon, which left a cloud of dust in its wake. Mariana asked Judith and Anne to look for White Moon and told the rest of the girls to wait there.

The wagon stopped near the school door and the principal went to greet the arrival with a big smile on her face. The shipment of money and provisions was then attended by Father Edward, the gardeners and three strong staff members, who took the provisions and goods to the basement. The large, heavy and secured pouch with the money was given to Mariana.

The men left quickly on the wagon, leaving notes for Father Edward, detailing where the money should be distributed and the needs of other schools.

Outside the school grounds, five thieves, with scarves covering their faces, hid behind large tree branches, carrying rifles and revolvers. Alan was their leader. One of the thieves on a galloping horse entered the school grounds and threw several lit torches through the windows of the school — one of them came in Mariana's direction. She froze, dropping the heavy pouch of money that she was going to take to her office. And Alan came galloping in, without qualms and with a revolver in his hand.

"Hands up, everyone. One false move and I'll blow your brains out of your good-for-nothing heads!"

The girls started screaming and running in all directions. A fire quickly started inside the school. Alan picked up the pouch from the ground and called his accomplices.

"Round up all the girls and tie them to the trees. Then go to the basement. Grab everything and put it in the school's wagon." One of the men grabbed Judith and slapped her face when she fought against him and tied her to a tree.

"Alan, untie me," she called to him. "This was not our deal."

With blood boiling in his face, he responded, "I don't know you, except that you are a stupid slut."

The priest, embarrassed and devastated on recognizing that the head of the robbers was his nephew, was stopped by a shot towards his foot.

White Moon now emerged out of hiding in her native clothing with a military rifle in her hand. She ran towards Alan, aiming it at him, and shouted, "Drop your gun or I'll shoot you. Release Mariana."

Alan was surprised to see an Indian holding a rifle more powerful than his. He recognized that it was White Moon. Mariana, also surprised to see Mariana, admired her courage. She covered her face with both hands. The girls were all shocked to see the unusual sight of an Indian risking her life to defend all of theirs. At that moment, lightning tore through the sky, and loud thunder brought more confusion, and it began to rain.

"Where the hell did you come from, you goddamn Indian?" Alan shouted indignantly. "I will not let Mariana go. All this money is mine." He shot at her, but she was able to dodge it. Taking a few steps to the right, she shot near Alan's right foot. Scared by the girl's courage and retribution, he let his rifle fall. White Moon ran and quickly disarmed him. But another thief came up from behind her and pulled the rifle from her hands.

Glad to see White Moon disarmed, Alan screamed, "You damn Indian, I want to see if you are able to face two men. Don't think I'll let this go easy. I will not let your affront go unpunished. After we have both beaten you as much as we can, I'll have the pleasure of killing you."

Alan did not know that he was stepping right into a trap.

White Moon, like a panther with the soul of a warrior, remembered what she had been taught by Ayana and did the "wolf's dance in front of them". She could move around them without letting herself be caught by them. They were unable to hold her and she was able to avoid them both. "Be careful!" Alan called out to his accomplice. "I don't know what this crazy girl is doing. She is as slippery as soap."

White Moon heard the loud thunder, and without a word or emotion, focused on the fighting and began to quickly strike blows on all sides. It was an unexpected and tense fight for the thieves. When one fell, another would get up and be beaten without pity, being hit by quick, decisive blows. Blood gushed from their noses, and they took kicks and punches all over their bodies. Alan fell near his gun, which was lying on the ground. With an effort, he tried to grab it.

White Moon quickly jumped and took the gun by the barrel and hit him hard on his head with the butt.

"To me, you are just two carcasses," she said out of breath. "You are worthless. Not even worthy of the air you breathe.

I want you both to know that I left fear in my mother's womb when she died."

Mary, now on the other side of the grounds, with a rifle in her hand, gathered up her courage and shot at one of the assailants and hit him in the arm. He fell, screaming in pain, and surrendered. Another thief quickly let go of the priest. All the girls screamed for help because the fires were now beginning to grow large in size.

"Thank God," Mariana said. "Thanks to White Moon's courage. We are all safe. Girls, fast! Get water — we need to put out the fires."

White Moon looked at Marina and said, "There are still two dangerous thieves in the basement, stealing provisions and loading them in the school's wagon round the corner."

Dazed, Mariana rubbed her head and said to a recovering Father Edward, "My God! I dropped the money in the chaos. Let's hide it behind the sculpture of the Virgin Mary. There's no time to go to my office now, we have to help to put the fires out."

White Moon was happy with the idea. "Yes!" she said "Run and recover the money" Meanwhile, Mary and I will go down to the basement with our guns to catch them both."

Father Edward took a short cut behind the school, run towards them carrying the pouch of money, he had retrieved. Mariana was surprised.

"Father, you were faster than me." The two of them ran to hide the heavy pouch behind the Madonna.

All the girls, now free, ran to get buckets and anything they could find to carry water from the little nearby stream. The flames were now growing quite large. Edwina shouted to organize all the girls and the staff.

White Moon and Mary, guns in their hands, hid behind a native plant and saw the two men stealing provisions and about to take them away in the school buggy. But Mary who was careless moved, and was caught by one of the thieves.

Near to the basement window, the other thief was terrified. He was carrying a large bag of groceries and unarmed when he saw White Moon. He dropped the bag and quickly grabbed a still-lit torch nearby, trying to burn her, but she kicked him. He didn't know that there was ammunition and weapons stored in the basement, and he dropped the torch right above a small barrel containing gunpowder. They were now near the door and continued fighting. After about a minute, there was an explosion, throwing him up in the air — everything was engulfed in flames. His clothes burned.

White Moon, being further away, was less affected by the explosion, but she was nevertheless very shaken and fainted. As she saw an angel of golden light emerge from a white cloud of smoke, she thought she was dead. She recognized her indigo blue eyes, for it was the same angel who had always appeared in her dreams when she was in distress and needed help. The angel read her thoughts and said, "I'm your Guardian Angel. You have not yet reached your time to go to another dimension. Go to your people and command the Cherokee Indians as the great warrior that God made you. You have fulfilled your destiny here. Take the knowledge you have acquired here, go to your tribe, and continue teaching the spiritual values of life and also Cherokee ancestry." The Angel of Light took White Moon in her arms and brought her out of the disaster.

Held in the strong and nurturing grip of her Guardian Angel, she realized that this was no longer the same Angel. It was Jesus — the man who was nailed to the cross, the man she wanted to meet, the man the priest spoke so much about — who was carrying her. Dressed in clothes of pure white, he had the most loving and sweet smile. He put White Moon in a field of emerald green grass full of lavender-scented flowers. He then said something very powerful.

"Amen, you are saved."

White Moon awoke from the dream and was near the hidden basement to the right side of the Virgin Mary's sculpture in the schoolyard. At that moment, Mother Nature reacted and even heavier rain fell, helping to quell the flames that were licking the school building.

"It is a miracle!" the priest said. Everyone gathered around

White Moon to see her safe at the feet of the Blessed Virgin Mary.

Meanwhile, Mary, who was barely able to breathe from the smoke, was able to free herself from the other thief and run out of the basement. He ran away, but the others were tied up and locked in a secure storeroom to wait for the authorities and their fate.

The heavy rain continued for several hours, but stopped when it began to get dark. Life always brings happy reverses of fortune.

With the clatter of horses' hooves, Utah came with Captain Andrew and several soldiers. They were shocked when they saw the disaster at the school, part of which had been destroyed by fire. Utah jumped down off his horse and ran to find White Moon. He found Mariana, who was holding White Moon's hand as they both walked towards him. She let go of her hand for her to run into the arms of her beloved. They hugged tightly, their hearts uniting in the love and happiness of the reunion.

He was so happy and filled with so much love and happiness that he asked, "White Moon, will you marry me?"

"Yes, of course," she said. "It is already written in the stars!" The captain was happy to see his friend's happiness.

"I received a message, warning about the assault on the school," he told his best friend Mariana. "Now that all is well, I think we should ask the priest to marry them as quickly as possible, to put out their fire," he joked. Everyone laughed at the captain's amusing words. Thinking about the lovers' happiness, the principal agreed and asked the priest to perform the ceremony as soon as possible the next day. Mariana and Captain Andrew would be the witnesses. Edwina would work overnight to bake a special wedding cake. All the girls would attend the wedding, and everyone would be happy.

The principal now happily housed the newlyweds at the school. Utah gratefully spoke to Mariana. "In a few days, White Moon will turn eighteen. I will take her to the Cherokee reservation where we'll begin a new life."

Thrilled, Mariana responded, a tear falling from the corner of her eye. "Of course! The wedding made it official. Be happy."

However, the surprises were not all over — after the ceremony, to the back of the school — where everyone was enjoying — through the rear entrance, came a carriage. A strange woman emerged, wearing dark robes, and appearing somewhat disheveled. She stepped out of the carriage and ran right into the newlyweds and the principal.

Mariana became irritated at this stranger's presence and wondered who she was: who would enter through the back gate and into the middle of a party?

"I'm Elvira, White Moon's guardian," she said. "She was adopted under the name Samira by my father, the late US Army Captain."

White Moon shuddered at her appearance and her words. Elvira continued, "Sorry I entered through the back gate. When I found out that the school had a fire, I became worried about her safety. I come in peace. I know that she will soon be eighteen, and I would like to take her to spend some time with me."

Captain Andrew came over to the group and recognized the impostor from a WANTED poster, who had sold information to other countries about the Cherokee's gold. He quickly approached her, taking out his gun and pointing it in the direction of the shrew. "Elvira," he said, "You are under arrest and will be brought to the US Supreme Court and judged for selling state information. Who would have thought? I have looked for you all over in many states, and here you are, like a rotten fish caught in a net. Should you resist, I can take you by force. You have to know that White Moon is now a married woman to Utah here — and you can do nothing more to her now."

Mariana, after hearing the whole story, was very scared and realized that Elvira was there to try to hurt White Moon yet again.

She now sensed that the time was right to set things straight with her niece. Judith, embarrassed at having been denounced by Alan, now, always walked with her head down. She did not know how her aunt would react. Mariana was steady and did not let herself be taken over by familiar feelings. She called the captain and denounced Judith and told him the whole truth. Alan and his accomplices were injured and were tied up and secured by the school's gardeners. They were awaiting their punishment. The captain sent for the girl, angry and upset by her wickedness and the severity of her acts against her own aunt and the other girls.

"Today, your lover, you, and all of those who participated in this horror will be taken with Elvira. I have caught all of the rotten fish in one fell swoop and will take them all to prison."

Elvira was distraught and cried out. Judith now joined the others who were all tied up and ordered into the military wagon with a canvas cover. The captain said goodbye to Mariana. She didn't want to cry, so she closed her eyes and left, carrying the heartache of having to turn in her own blood relative who had become so rotten.

The next day, the golden sun brought the blessings of light and happiness. White Moon, assuming again her Native American identity, put on more of beautifully decorated new clothes that Utah had brought for her as gifts.

Utah took White Moon in his strong arms and put her in his carriage. Mariana and Father Edward and all the school clapped for the couple. They both thanked them for teaching them the truth about the Cherokee Indians and for the fact that she had the courage to defend everyone with her own life. The whole school, with their thanks for her courage and best wishes, came out to send them on their way to their new life of happiness.

In a miracle of life that could be felt by all who were present, the scent of lavender and roses, issued from the love of Jesus, took over the lovers' path.

White Moon and Utah were victorious. AMEN!

About the Author

'Amazing Stories from times gone by
'Revealed through my Spiritual Dreams'

Vera Lucia Lima

Born into a large Catholic family in São Paulo, Brazil, aged about 12, I could see and hear things others couldn't, and agonized about sharing these visions with my family and repressive educators. I started a new life in Australia, aged 18 - married and had a family. My amazing spiritual dreams, all set in the past were 'channeled' and 'revealed' to me over several months - of people and places of which I had no knowledge. Writing these episodes down, I was able to create my books.

My two books have powerful spiritual messages that fascinate and reward my readers – worldwide with a true spiritual connection.

Other books by Vera Lucia Lima:

https://www.amazon.com/Vera-Lucia-Lima/e/B01HYUQ12Y
amazon.com/author/veralima

Made in the USA
Middletown, DE
26 October 2021

51105775R00086